subtle bodies

SUBTLE
BODIES

A Fantasia on Voice, History and René Crevel

PETER
DUBÉ

Lethe Press • *Maple Shade, New Jersey*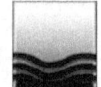

Published in 2010 by LETHE PRESS, INC.
118 Heritage Avenue ♦ Maple Shade, NJ 08052-3018
www.lethepressbooks.com ♦ lethepress@aol.com
ISBN: 1-59021-330-0
ISBN-13: 978-1-59021-330-8

This is a work of fiction. Names, characters, places, and incidents are products of the author's imagination or are used fictitiously.

Set in Jenson, Savoye, & Perpetua.
Cover image: Mathieu Beauséjour.
Cover and interior design: Alex Jeffers.

LIBRARY OF CONGRESS
CATALOGING-IN-PUBLICATION DATA

Dubé, Peter, 1962-
 Subtle bodies : a fantasia on voice, history and René Crevel / Peter Dubé.
     p. cm.
 ISBN-13: 978-1-59021-330-8 (pbk. : alk. paper)
 ISBN-10: 1-59021-330-0 (pbk. : alk. paper)
 1. Crevel, René, 1900-1935--Fiction. 2. Poets, French--20th century--Fiction. 3. Surrealism (Literature)--France--Fiction. 4. Suicide--Fiction. I. Title.
 PR9199.4.D82S83 2010
 813'.6--dc22

                    2010018786

As always, for Mathieu, with love.

Does happiness arise from blows given or blows received, and unhappiness from those that were not given, those that were not received? It's a strange question to ask, eyelids closed, when you have just asked the June sun, the glacier's air, for the most intimate and most solitary metamorphosis.

RENÉ CREVEL
My Body and I

BODIES
OF SPEECH

When the door closes behind me, it is almost soundless.

Why does that surprise me? Why shouldn't something, at least, be silent.

There. There. Sliding Door. One that revolves. A door that opens onto another. There. Too. A door that moves to the sound of music. There are many kinds of door; there will be more.

I walk into the apartment without turning on a light. It's better that way; too much happens in the light. Friends turn on one another; reputations are ruined, powerful men crush the less so under their heels, dreams are destroyed, shattered past repair. All that happened today. All that happened in broad daylight. Right now, it feels as if the crimes of darkness are a little less cruel because less reasoned, less deliberate. Though I know the feeling will pass.

That is the greatest sadness of any feeling – that it passes.

Even without a burning bulb, in my mind's eye, I see my rooms with perfect clarity. The bookshelves on one wall, my friends' paintings on the other, the little drawing of a half-naked sailor that J. did hanging by the closet door. My armchair with the green silk cushions, the table beside it on which rests last night's empty bottle of Pastis, six white sea shells, a bronze coffin nail with a death's head embossed on the end, and the small, lacquered foot of some infant reptile a friend brought back for me from one of his more eccentric voyages. This room contains all my treasures: memories and fears. The darkness does nothing to hide them. So, perhaps it is not as innocent as I would like to think. No innocence in either light or dark. I turn on the electricity.

Electricity still has the power to startle me. Born with the century, I can recall rooms lit with gas growing up. A half-light that might favor cruelties bright and dark. Both of which my Mother was happy to indulge; she was such a hard woman. Inflexibly middle class, hubristic, obsessed with propriety.

I know, with great discomfort, the future will be dominated by the unblinking illumination of electricity, that whole worlds, entire ways of life, will be made possible by it while others will be wiped away; that whims will be transformed into necessities, rivers rerouted, lands submerged, all in the interest of casting out shadow, making every minute of every day lucid, clear, sensible…profitable. Soon this cold, steady light will stop being a mere service, it will be the world itself, men and women labouring for it, worshipping at its altar to endless productivity. In its relentless glow, secrets will be banished, private lives nullified, they will become the victims of a perpetual gaze made possible by the thrumming labyrinth of power lines and buried cables. A whole universe created only to be presided over by a terrible and artificial eye. It is sad and ridiculous. But, it will be. I know that much.

There's a little Pastis left in the bottle. I pour it, and walk into the kitchen. The mirror on the wall is coated in dust. I haven't cleaned it in weeks and weeks.

I turn the gas on. Open the oven door, draw a tiny heart in the dust and avoid looking in the newly exposed glass. I push back the fear that a vision might appear; it never does despite all the promises of legend. With me, it's always a voice. And on the rare moments the sound is accompanied by a mental image, it is short-lived and never as concrete as a reflection in a mirror, it's a more wavering, watery image. Hardly worth commenting on. But the voices on the other hand, they are substantial.

Yes. Yes. There will be images too. Floods of them sufficient to topple towers, raze civilizations. There. And there again. Small images in the corners of space; a girl picking out her wedding dress, a victim of violence bleeding from one ear, unable to speak for the swelling of his mouth and bitten tongue, an engineer struggling with the tensile strength of a new metal. And larger too, the map, topographical and somewhat speculative of oceanic trenches, state portraits made a span of months before a given dictator topples, the gain and loss of weight by

*famous faces. All such images crowding us in, crowding out our
silences. And light to make them by. And darkness to see them
in. Scopophilic currencies are coined to traffic in the optical.
On the walls of tall buildings you will place…*

Yes, voices like that, here to trouble me again. I refuse to rise
to the bait.

Instead I sip my drink and admonish myself for being foolish. The truth is I don't leave the mirror dusty for fear of visions. I'm not worried about any spirits or apocalyptic signs. I
just don't want to see myself in it. I'm sure the day's stress and
pain are clear on my face and I can't stand the visible signs of
despair. There were moments today I could literally hear my
heart breaking.

The day must have been hard on André too. I'm sure he's
heard every detail of it. And I'm sure he hid his feelings from
every prying eye. André is too proud to show shame or sadness.
He is always too proud.

I can still remember the first time I met him. Remember it
so clearly. It was more than a decade ago now, though in many
ways I was more than ten years younger then. I was young
enough to endure a divided life.

In those days, the split I had to live with was simpler; I was
a student-soldier. My situation brought on by the war and its
ending – a kind of sudden solution to national need, cobbled
together on the fly, a way of dealing with the young men re-
turning from the front. I spent my mornings at the university,
studying the great tradition of French literature and its centu-
ries of lights, and my afternoon and evening in the barracks,
doing what young men in barracks have undoubtedly done
since barracks were invented. We muddled through training,
marches, parades and drills, the endlessly repeated calisthenics.
We tried to keep from accidentally shooting each other.

In those cramped quarters, my closest friend was M.; there
was so much character in his round little form. The light shone
off his glasses –a nearly-moist gleam, like the moon lifting into

the sky – as he clambered over the garrison wall on his way
to some nocturnal rendezvous. And, like the moon, he soared
over our barrack's wall every night.

I can remember the conversations we shared in that nasty little dormitory, the only thing that made the weeks, the months,
livable. Long talks, late into the night, always about books and
poets. The kind of books and poets that aren't taught in university classrooms. Violent, passionate poets, half-mad poets, lustful and riotous poets. Bards of insurrection and fiery destruction. The poets of desire in its most obscure forms: singing
of drugs and torments, lascivious statuary, fornicating sharks,
every kind of beautiful monstrosity. We talked and talked and
talked about them, praised their verses until sunrise, rhapso-
dized their dark nights of the soul through countless nights
of our own. Once under the oak in our courtyard M., home
before dawn for once and drunk, picked up the point of some
empty shell and put it on his head – a crooked miter. He began to recite some blasphemous lines from Baudelaire while
gesticulating with his left hand. The rest of us knelt and took
sips from cheap wine between intoning our responses. At some
point in our ritual, we fell asleep on the ground.

And so we sealed our friendship, we student-soldiers, and
opened the vaults of our many secrets (all laughable now.) M.
and the lurid accounts of his conquests. Someone poured out
his jealousy of his younger brother. The other fellows shared
fears and aspirations. I raged against my Mother's cruelties, her
sacrifice of any tenderness to her position, my father's end. I
alone may have raised some eyebrows in my raging against my
family. So be it.

Looking back on so much love so quickly won, it seems to me
that such intimacy is only possible for young men in military
service. I've never known it to happen anywhere else. I believe
it is possible in arms not for any of the obvious – and hope-
lessly moralizing– reasons most often cited to account for it. It
has nothing to do with camaraderie, or *esprit de corps*. Nothing

to do with shared danger, certainly, since most of barracks life, at least during those rare times of peace, is – to the contrary – shared boredom. No, I think the rapid closeness was possible because we were thrown together in our frightened lonely youth, caught in an unreal time and a place that had nothing to do with our actual lives, with the shape and the direction they might take. And lost in that terrible limbo, we clung to any kindred spirit to give shape, some semblance of meaning, to the void. It was inevitable that we should become friends, those men, like me, loved the inexhaustible vitality and pleasure of words. A group of us even established a little magazine to publish the violent, glittering anti-social kind of writing that thrilled us. The title? "Adventure."

We were young.

And, to circle back to where I began, it was through *Adventure* that I would come to meet André. The first time I met him I was with the grandiosely named "Editors" of *Adventure*. We had attended one of the evenings of provocation that his gang of young writers scheduled with regularity, and subsequently, been invited to one of their meetings. We met them at the Cêrta, a café so unfashionable as to have reclaimed a certain glamour; it had begun to serve "avant-garde" cocktails. The zinc of the counter-top was so scuffed and scratched it appeared moiré.

I first sighted André at a table with his intimates. I would be less than entirely truthful if I did not confess at the start that the man struck me immediately – and powerfully. I spotted him the moment I passed through the doors. Saw him, as if he were alone, separate from the crowd surrounding him. His bearing was precise, the shoulders squared, the chin raised. He had a mass of dark hair brushed off a strong brow and his gaze raked across the crowd, the whole room, like a beam of powerful, dazzling light. I could tell at once that he missed nothing. And he had an inescapable presence, a field of magnetic energy, around him. The man could bring the volume of raucous conversation down with a gesture. He seemed to me an archangel, a sword-wielding seraph guarding the doors to paradise, some unfathomable kingdom of delight, of knowledge, and of marvels.

Of course, I thought he was extraordinarily handsome.

He rose to shake our hands as we approached. That cool, appraising glance fell across me. I greeted him, and he corrected my formality smiling, saying, "Please, call me André," in a manner that was at once charming and unnerving. He held onto my hand the whole time. He grinned again, insisted that all of us forego any bourgeois protocol and gestured for us to join the group in their tumult.

And what tumult it was. The group around André took the late night barracks exchanges of my friends and me to dizzying levels. I had never heard talk like this, and – despite the years in which I was integral to the group – no other conversation has dazzled me in the same way since.

The first time a young man finds himself in company like this, awash with a passion for ideas, alive to the fire of words, is unique; it's a kind of a first love, a great, blood-deep desire to know and experience. It churns and is unsatisfiable, but it transports you. It turned my world on its head. To say I was ready for it would be too soft: I was aching for it.

The old world vanished the moment I was seated. The university, the niggling maternal miseries, certainly my military service. It all meant nothing. Ordinary life meant nothing. For a few hours we plotted a wholesale transformation of the world. In shouts and laughter we covered a chaos of thought, image, intellect. The group spoke of: the mechanical specifics of certain articulated doll heads made at the end of the last century, tribal art from Melanesia, the viability of "propaganda of the deed," the breeding habits of a particular species of dragonfly, the differences between Greek and Roman versions of mythology, the painting of Francis Picabia, the progress of the Russian revolution, the differences in quality of the brothels off the

Rue St. Denis, the stylistic strengths of a line of popular novels about the crimes of an underworld lord, the performance of Camille, a fashionable cabaret singer, the price of apartments in the 11th *arrondisement*, poetry, lots and lots of poetry. And the plans for an upcoming "Congress" among writers and intellectuals that was in the works.

My head spun.

There's a clatter down on the street. I can hear it despite the shut windows, some shouting from the street. A man's voice... definitely a man's voice. He is cursing at someone, angry about a price being asked. His voice is deep, accented. It reminds me a bit of the American poet I spent a summer with years ago. The Sun Worshipper we called him. He was beautiful and almost pagan. He loved pleasure. I will miss moments like those. That is all I will miss.

You are too quick. There will be moments for which no words yet exist. Why such precipitiousness? There are, and will be, ways of living still unconceived of. Pleasures and transformations to be learned. There – a whole generation of youth, blood hot with hunger and with need, throw themselves into their bodies and each others': tasting, touching, teasing out sensations and when it's done still needing more. There – they gather in an open field, or a clearing in a wood, or on a steep, clean slope. They come together brightly costumed, some playing flutes or drums, or stringed instruments; they make a music mated to their manias. Some carry tools: shovels and hammers and saws or else long, sturdy posts in wood. They come together in the world's open places. Spaces that are sufficient to the act of love, to see, to hear, to long. And they begin to build. Digging into the cool, dark earth, setting up the fine sanded-smooth wooden posts as the sky grows full, dark clouds assemble overhead. Their labors done, they disrobe; show graceful, pale nakedness in the grey air, the deepening chill. Some among them help a friend or lover to a post and taking up a coiled length of rope, begins to bind him there. And still the music-mak-

ers play, sending slim vibrations into the tense and turbulent
air. Trills. Tremors. A slow, repeating line of percussion. The
clouds move down, lowering themselves. Their knots complete,
the binders kiss their friends and turn to shout towards the sky.
They raise their voices and hurl imprecations, crying out to the
gathering storm, begging its arrival. They howl and scream,
they sing and intone frenzied, spontaneous verses, summoning
wind, and rain, and violent thunder. And it comes, the weather
comes. With deliberate pace and a kind of grim ceremony the
wind rises, a rolling bass echoes overhead and the first drops
begin to fall. The chanting officiants laugh and redouble their
invocations. They succeed. The storm breaks in the heavens,
a terrible wind rushes over field, through woods and up every
slope in the eager, lustful world. The naked bodies tied to the
posts arch their backs and moan. Their bellies and their back
are lashed by rain; they sigh. The wind pummels their flesh,
drawing blood to the surface and the cool flow of water runs
over their genitals, stiffening, engorging, ready for the touch.
They cry out for their elemental lovers while their partners
keep the music and the song in play. The bound youths give
themselves over to the touch of the world with bliss, with blind,
hungry ecstasy. The roar of the storm builds. And builds some
more; the drums and flutes and singers are drowned in the
deafening noise. Crying out, the lewd victims set their tongues
free as at last, at last the lighting opens the sky. They shout
all their secrets, every hidden desire for the joy of speaking it,
the blind hope that the tempest will take them there and give
them this unspeakable pleasure. No one in all the crowd hears
anything but the wind and the joy around them. No one will
ever know of this.

Shut up. Shut up. This is neither time nor place. I am not
at my bliss, and I know no transcendence in my storm. I have
known too many storms by far.

Indeed tumult – and betrayals – lay ahead. André's congress,
so eagerly discussed that evening, was, it's safe to assume, at

least partially designed to ensure he held an important place in radical artistic circles – to make him more prominent. Though it never occurred, the plans and politicking around the attempt did move him closer to the centre of things. It also provoked much resentment among certain writers and intellectuals. Despite this, and though my hesitation in taking a side did not pass unnoticed, it did not turn André against me. I grew closer to his group, even publishing some of them in the pages of *Adventure*. That decision to publish may have cemented my contact with André. In the days following the issue's appearance I lunched with him. He thanked my colleagues and me for accepting his friends' poems, and made a passionate speech about the value of community among writers committed to changing literature, and changing the place and role of literature in the world. As he spoke his face went very white, his eyes shone; even the timbre of his voice altered, as if some terrible spirit was struggling to break through his flesh. Every word seemed charged with *knowledge*, an assurance of what it meant. I listened intently. When we rose from the table to leave, André slipped me an envelope saying it was a token of his appreciation. It held a letter, a warm letter: one I have kept as a memory of those early days of our friendship, and it contained a little gift. An old, nineteenth-century, playing card: the Jack of Diamonds. He had drawn on it, altering the figure's face. Drawing a sort of nimbus around the head, that suggested a blend of human eye and halo. At the top he had written the words "see everything." I smiled at it. But I didn't know why.

I spent the summer following this first encounter on the coast, a holiday that gave me the time to think through my relationship with my new friends and the life I wanted once I was free of my studies and my military service. The life of a writer. It was good to be away from Paris, from its feuding, its blandishments and array of pleasures. Those I had already discovered and those still waiting to be explored.

For the first week or so I found the blank regularity of sand and waves reassuring. I thought nothing could trouble me there, at the heart of so much emptiness. It was all empty space for new things to grow, air and light that might make anything possible. I can still see the garishly orange sky as the day ended, still hear the sound of the wind, raucous and reassuring. The smell of salt was filled with rough wonder. Even the company of my family was insufficient to deaden the pleasure of the place.

Though meals were a family matter, I had enough time alone, and enough ways to fill it. I would spend mornings reading and afternoons walking along the beach, or swimming. I would spend some evenings hard at work on the pieces I had begun to publish in literary magazines, the faint beginnings of a reputation.

I walked the beach one day and saw the sky darken. Clouds were heavy and the sea choppy with small, stiff points. A bracing bite took the air despite the August date, reminding me of summer's end and my return to Paris. I passed an orchard that grew near the coast. The smell of ripening fruit, the gold and green of apples and the silver of pears was thick. Their fleshy perfumes mated with the salt air rousing appetite and attention, sharpening every sense. I rounded a rocky point and saw, in my peripheral vision, a movement in the sand, something out of place, grey and white and mobile against the different shades of grey and white in the sand. A fluttering. A large seabird lay in the sand, its wings spread to their full span; only the head moved, turning right and left, the beak opened and shut with no apparent rhythm. It bent down to poke in the sand. I walked towards the creature. Its only response was to turn toward me and let out a harsh cry. I came closer, the head bobbed up and down and he cried once more. I slowed my approach; the wings stayed motionless. In a moment or two, he returned to his piercing of the ground beneath him. I took a few more steps and he was off. The bird took to the air almost instantly, with hardly a beat of those broad wings. A small point vanishing against a horizon in full fugue. Where he had lain, there were only small disturbances in the sand. A pattern, an almost perfect spiral, oval and growing tighter as it circled in. I had never seen anything like that.

The next day, on an impulse, I walked back to the same spot. The pattern was gone, wiped away by the tide. And the bird too was absent. I stood for a moment looking out at the ocean, then up at the sky, loving both for the simple blankness. Then I heard a voice behind me.

"Good afternoon," it said. One of those blank greetings: question or affirmation? I turned around. A girl...or a young woman. Perhaps eighteen. She was pretty, bright looking, with a strange presence; she was completely involved simply saying "hello," bending forward, putting her whole body into the greeting. She said "hello" like it was a whole conversation, or a negotiation. We talked for a while: small talk, the aimless, pleasurable divagations of young people on holiday. It was agreeable to both of us I think. Neither made any haste to bring the talk to an end, at any rate. Soon enough the ordinary exchanges took on odder dimensions. We shared confidences that, when I took my leave of her, felt surprising. Things about my family, my dreams, my anger. None of it fazed her and, when it was done, she invited me to her mother's that evening. Caught off-guard by our little exchange, I said "yes."

I had reason to second-guess my precipitous acceptance when I entered the house that evening. The living room was laden with esoteric bric-a-brac; incense burners and dark mirrors, astrological charts and strange carvings, celestial globes and heavy candlesticks, weighty, richly-bound tomes, something I could have sworn was a wand or a scepter, and a great, glittering ball of crystal. Taking pride of place in all of this imposing clutter was Madame Dante.

Madame Dante was an old woman, grey-haired, with a portentous, raspy voice that was given to making hierophantic pronouncements. After the introductions were made she exclaimed, "Tonight there shall be incantations!"

With that, we were all called to gather in the dining room, where, in anticipation, the table had been draped with a scarlet cloth. We took our seats, joined hands and *La Dante* began the aforementioned incantations. But that is all I recall, directly, of the events.

The young lady and her mother later told me that within moments my head fell to the table in a trance. They described to me the utterances I made: crazy things, visions of other times and places, mysterious voices coming through me, prophecies. But I had seen or heard none of it myself. I couldn't remember one of my inspired messages. It was a blank – and it has remained one ever since.

Shortly after my grand initiation, my leave ended and I returned to Paris, and to the barracks, slightly shaken by my summer but still intact. Not long after that, I saw André again, who still seemed as ready as I to let the kerfuffle over his failed "Congress" slide. We spent an afternoon together on a *terasse* and my bedazzled first impression was confirmed. He was charming and engaging. The conversation was extravagant, ranged over everything. He told me about the excitement he felt for the automatic writing he and his friends had undertaken. The treasure trove of startling, bizarre, erotic and disturbing images they had discovered, and how obsessive they had become about them. And he recounted their exploration of dreams as well. He was passionate, serious; he leaned in close to talk to me, and I felt the same dizzy certainty in his utterances as I had our last meeting. With every word his hidden currents tugged at my own. He touched my hand at one point, stressing a point. Then he said, he was eager to hear what I had been doing, where "my most vital passions lay."

Hesitant at first, stuttering at the risk of seeming foolish, I told him about the seance at the beach. André slapped the table and pounced on the idea. He shouted out; trances of this sort would fit perfectly among the experiments already underway. With great excitement he invited me to recreate the events at his home. And, once again, I accepted.

He walked with me to a mutually convenient *metro* station after our long, labyrinthine conversation. As we strolled along the *Rue du Temple* he told me how happy he had been with our first meeting last spring. How closely he had read an issue or two of *Adventure*. He stopped on a corner, and with eyes half-shut, told me how he had known since he was a boy that a new spirit was moving in the world; how he'd sworn to be a part of it – a spirit of daring creativity, committed to the most radical transformation of what it could mean to be human, fully human. He told me that the instant he read some of my texts he knew that I too was a part of this vast "adventure." And he winked at the silly pun as he shook my hand again, saying goodbye at the top of the stairs to the platform. I am sure I blushed.

The following Monday I arrived at his studio with eagerness and no idea what might occur. André's wife, S., showed me into an extraordinary room. It was inhabited by *things*. Books stood on shelves and piled in corners; little matchboxes with childlike paintings from the earliest years of the century were aligned on tables, dolls lounged atop one shelf, on his desk I could see a kabalistic necklace and a wooden snuff box in the shape of a frog. On a side board there was a collection of tromp l'oeil bottles, one of them covered in dominos and up against a corner, four or five walking sticks on which deaths' heads, demons' heads, the skulls of birds rested, awaited use. There were decks of cards, and tiny figurines, a strange lance from some far off island, and, of course, paintings, (though fewer than there would be later.) There were manuscripts stacked up or bound. The room was filled with more real wonders than Mme. Dante could have conjured up in her wildest imaginings. Everywhere one looked something was ready to ravish or torment the eye. And in the midst of it all, was an equally extraordinary-looking young man named R. who had large, liquid, staring eyes. S. brought me to André who was with him, waiting, and clearly pleased with my arrival. We chatted very briefly, but – though attentive and courtly as ever – my host was clearly chewing at the bit. He was desperate to get down to business. S., sensing her husband's anxiousness, discreetly suggested we sit down, pointing towards the table. André seized on the opportunity, "Yes. Yes. René, I believe we should sit in a circle for the experiment, no?"

"Yes," I replied. I outlined what I remembered of my seance on the coast. The position we adopted, the strange mumbled invocations of Madame Dante. And, as I did, I felt myself flush, and my stomach turn over. I began to sweat. The fact was I remembered almost nothing of that night; I had fallen into some state of unconsciousness and was only told later of what happened.

The skin around my eyes felt tight. I felt hot. What if I did not fall into a trance tonight? All of these people were here to hear me utter oracles. I had no idea if I could do so. I might fail. I might shatter this renewed friendship with André. The pit of my stomach roiled at the thought of my humiliation, the contempt and laughter that alone could greet my failure. And the consequences of that were enormous. I sweat; my breath grew ragged. Friendships evaporating. The chances of publication, of the solace of other writers with whom to linger over cups of coffee and plot the future of our collective dreams dwindled and grew transparent. I saw a great, dark gulf underneath the table we were seated at.

S. dimmed the lights. I felt André on my left, and a German painter I did not know on my right, take hold of my hands. Our host, at my instruction, spoke a few soothing words of invitation to the air, and we awaited our visitation.

I felt nothing. I sat in silence, hoping, and waiting, and longing, imploring, I would have prayed, had I any faith at all, for *something*, some spectral voice, the touch of an ectoplasmic hand, a visionary door thrown open, to unleash a torrent of unheard-of images, but nothing. Nothing at all. My head was a vast, desert cavern, echoing with the unspoken.

All around me I felt the anticipation. No one moved. No chair shuffled. The intake of breath was shallow and infrequent. All attention was focused on what was before us, what had yet to be recognized as a void.

The turmoil in my guts worsened and my face felt licked with fire. I had no idea what to do, shame fell over me and I saw the end of my career hurtling down, an asteroid dropping from space. Did no one else see any of this?

Every moment that crept by was a blow on a gong. I ached in my bones and in my synapses. Unable to go on – I spoke.

I let out a sigh. Then another. I followed it with a shrill little shout. I had no idea where I was going. I just could not bear the silence, the sticky sensation of shame that clung to my flesh and clothing. Desperate, I improvised a bent narrative about a woman murdering her husband. Drowning him. Then leavened it with exclamations about frogs. And madness. I wove in bits of nonsense alliteration, and fragments that came to me spontaneously. Fabulous fraud. I spoke whatever came to hand out of terror and disgrace.

Then I opened my eyes and shook myself, breaking the circle. André stared at me wide-eyed. He was astounded. Thrilled. He congratulated me heartily, decried our failure to make a record of the proceedings, insisting it would have been an "invaluable document," a record of an immaterial state of being. He could hardly contain the torrent of enthusiasm. He insisted on repeating the experiment again, for more of the group, and in two days time. I laughed, hoping it didn't sound nervous. Agreed. Drinks were served. I could breathe again.

That night, in my room, the sheer idiocy of my actions overtook me. I was ready to bang my head against a wall. I could fool a couple of people who wanted to see something miraculous, but a room full of viewers with varying degrees of investment in the undertaking? Who knew what could be done in that context. And that is without considering the ethical difficulties of such a deception; it was all a lie, after all. Indefensible. I was so tense, so anxious that my legs trembled as I lay on my cot trying to find something reasonable to tell myself. My mind raced, running through hundreds of different answers, different possibilities and permutations. None of them offered any comfort. I tossed and turned. I rested on one side and then the other. I traced invisible lines between the patches of paint on the barrack's walls, imagining journeys to places far removed from that magical little apartment.

At length, in order to fake some faint peace of mind, I reminded myself that I had created my oracular speech spontaneously, from the dark places of my mind and soul; how far was that from these poets' much loved automatic writing? How distant from "real" mediumship? I had knit together my weird images, my fractured sentences and rollicking assonances without any conscious thought at all. Surely that in itself was some sort of otherworldly transmission. It had to be. Marvels come from somewhere too, I repeated to myself. Perhaps I had done what I pretended to have done. I said it over and over, a sad nursery rhyme that, after much effort, lulled me to something like the arms of sleep.

Perhaps I had done what I pretended to have done.

That refrain would stick in my mind until I returned to the scene of the crime. When I reached the top of the stairs, I found the tiny apartment filled with people. Besides our hosts and R., there were P., the German painter, another P. and his companion G. This time, André made little attempt at the social niceties. He allowed us a brief handshaking interlude and herded us unceremoniously toward the table. Those who were expected to enter a trance were seated, while a few observers hung back. The lights went down.

Once again, the terror fell over my head and shoulders, a great, dark pall. Once again, I felt empty; nothing came from whatever quiet place inside of me it was supposed to arise. Even worse, I couldn't improvise a single word. None of the stories that flowed so easily forty-eight hours earlier showed themselves to me. I could feel tears coming on. Then, I heard it. Not much. Just a single word: "there." I heard a voice very distinctly say "there." Then I heard it again. "There. There." It was a word of comfort, as a parent might offer a child with skinned knees. An exhortation too, a calling out, a pointing to a breach in a wall, or some other opening. It was more. Then it repeated. once, twice, three times in succession: "There. There. There." And each repetition was accompanied by a bright flash of light against the backs of my closed lids, in the hollow of my skull. Flashes of light and the word, the direction? Perhaps. The Exclamation, "there."

A brief space of silence and the voice came back. "*There. It is there. Look there. Your sought-after signal, your woman with her axe.*" And a rush, a flood of words and images came through me so fast, so dazzling I could not keep up. I saw and heard whole worlds in a space of time I couldn't hold on to. So many words and images and things and…experiences. Lives, whole lives, whole worlds. But I was awakened by André's hand passing over my face. I awoke to see him radiant with emotion. If it is possible, he was more thrilled than the last time.

The rush of chatter from the group almost rivaled the flood from which I was emerging, wet with weird images. They told me what I had channeled. Naked women brandishing axes. Scenes of murder and chaos. Adultery and betrayal. And though some of it rang familiar to me, it felt partial, incomplete. I had heard and seen so much more than I had spoken. And none of it felt as exhilarating and as *intimate* as what I'd been through. The things I had spoken though complex, playful, ambiguous and offering a glimpse of something, someplace else… were partial. What I had experienced was different; I'd heard things simultaneously, as if parts of me were elsewhere, other places or times, directed there by mysterious guides and voices.

Or rather, as if they took me to different places and times all at once. Like I was multiple, almost infinite bodies made of subtler stuff than flesh and blood that could move through walls and buildings, water and trees, through space, through time itself while talking to, hearing from, an infinite number of other people, and everyone of those hearing, seeing, listening forms all still remained me. Every one of those subtle bodies was coterminous with this one. And I discovered from my friends' reports on awakening that this poor fleshly form still had all its limitations and could only describe one thing at a time. Hence the strange and fragmentary narrative. The broken threads and dead ends of the discursive tapestry I'd known.

Of course none of my audience knew that. They only knew what I could tell them, and that was enough to please. They were passionately ready to continue the experiment; R. wanted to attempt the trance next, and in the charged atmosphere of the room, he fell into a sleep readily enough.

His head slumped forward, hung loosely from his shoulders. Then with stiff, marionette movements his hands began to scratch at the table. Little clawing gestures. Then they stopped as abruptly as they'd begun. R.'s head swung slightly, his back bent, then fell still. For a few seconds, and a few seconds more. The passing time seemed protracted, slowly dissolving over a stretch longer than the actual beat of the clock. Then suddenly his hands clawed at the table again, more violently. Rough, raking gestures. Every eye in the room turned to those hands, their violently agitated shaking. Out of some perversity, I turned to observe his slumped, sleeping head and – for the briefest of moments – I swear I saw his eyes flicker, scan the room for reaction quickly, then shut once again. I am almost certain of it.

A few moments later R. spoke a few rich, irrational sentences and spontaneously fell out of trance to find the room stunned. Bewildered.

I couldn't help but wonder if R. too, faced with failure had to chosen to feign success. One can't know. And either way, that night's seances opened the floodgates. André wanted more and more of these "sleeps." Wanted more and more access to the mysterious other worlds.

Over the weeks and months that followed, we gathered almost daily. The group would come together to storm the hidden places of the mind. And night after night the trances would come on, would deepen. For hours R. and I, and occasionally others, would go under and bring back glittering pearls from the deeps: pearls both bright and black. And each time, every new night, the trances grew more and more excessive.

Early on, in response to another of R.'s table-scratching sessions, I suggested that perhaps he wanted to write something down, eager to see what he might do with that. Immediately, he began to scribble down bizarre phrases, dated and annotated, snatches of unheard conversations, doodles and horrible scenes from a childlike inferno. And so the trances were joined to our already established interest in automatic writing. My new colleague caught the ball I tossed him with great verve and effectiveness. In later sessions he penned fabulous nonsense texts equating the poets in the group with varieties of plants and landmarks. In no time at all he was my chief rival in the macabre undertaking. And the stakes kept rising. Entranced members of the group would get up from their seats and stalk the corridors of our friends' apartments or our patrons' fashionable homes murmuring visionary alexandrines under their breath. People would see the dead rise again. Trees would grow upside down and the winged statues standing guard at the *Opéra Garnier* would piss on passers-by. In time, I could remember some of the declamations to emerge from all the tumult of my hypnogogic states, like the time I prophesied death and disease for some of my friends. Within days of the utterance, the German painter was in bed at home, coughing up blood. I sat in my darkened apartment, facing a wall for a week, after that. Happily, he pulled through.

The chaos grew and grew. There was the evening one of the sleepers locked us all in a room and vanished. How the panic built that night, the acrid smell clinging and cloying as we wondered, silently, if we had finally gone too far. There were long stretches in which the visions would grow darker and darker, wallowing in terror and in sadism.

One night R. (was he genuinely entranced, was he still faking, caught up in a dangerous game?) threatened us with a knife. Backing us up against a wall while he gestured, an irregular, shuddering motion, with the shining blade.

The fear in the group mounted, outstripped only by our fascination with the seances. We talked of nothing else. Every one of us believed that we were digging deeper into the buried roots of the mind and soul than anyone had ever gone before. Each of us felt that just one or two more sessions and real, transcendent marvels would reveal themselves. We lived for them; we rushed to every meeting; we slept very little, ate even less. We grew thin, our faces hollowed out, dark patches circled our eyes, framing a distant, distracted glassiness. Any risk was justified by the thought that we were close, so close to the absolute. We were not merely willing; we were desperate to gamble everything for such a reward.

And certainly, though fearful, I was too. Night after night my visions grew deeper, wider, more complex.

As I "slept" my subtle emanations recounted the buzz and business of hundreds of other worlds. Teeming, living worlds that were filled with life and passion. Their contours would blur, sliding across time and space. One moment it was a far off star, a dry desert world circling it, the next a distant future on this blue planet. Sometimes those things would blend together, glorious hybridity whose meaning was impossible to discern. I heard brief glimpses, saw fugitive images, flickering vistas. My subtler selves held long talks with disembodied interlocutors who dwelled in them and harvested their stories. All of this, all at once. And for the span of a sleep they were real, as real, as palpable as André, P., G.... As any of them. And they were amazing.

Once a voice came to me whispering of revolution, of young people taken to the streets and giddy with rage and laughter and lust. Intoxicated they would sing before policemen and cast flowers at armies. With broad grins they followed flowers with rocks, smashed the windows of banks and set vehicles aflame for the glory of it. I heard long, meandering accounts of barricades set up in the street, of workers fleeing their places of employment to join the transfigured people of the streets. I heard snatches of the songs they sang: loud, clamorous, played on instruments still to be invented, with rhythms of overwhelming power, insistent, coarse – and melodies as sinuous as eels crawling atop each other in a barrel. I heard stories of pitched battles fought in the twilight of shattered street lamps, of orgies joined in the vacated battlefields. In one long stretch of history, I heard the tale of young man who gathered friends around him to plot a total transformation of human life. Of their long nights of conspiring and days of mind-crushing meetings. The voice giggled as it shifted from this to his long slow suicide, accomplished by bottles of whiskey and deep embitterment. The visiting voice described scenes of grim hope lit and subsequently crushed and from time to time I saw quick, bright images of it: streets that might have been Paris, but not the Paris I knew. Brilliant with color day and night, more peopled than I could conceive, on every corner, young men with great manes and murder in their eyes piling up debris to shut down the streets of St. Germain, machinery called in to oppose them. Then there were voices on the air, brittle and at vast volumes, ripping through the branches of the oaks along the boulevards. It was beautiful and horrible and I can still remember so much of this account. But this is the first I've spoken of it.

In a different sleep another voice came, this one more sensual, with an impossible tale. A whole civilization, this time dedicated to tunnels. A world obsessed with a single project,

the elaboration of subterranean passages in a precise, prede-
termined pattern, the complete graphic representation of their
cosmological system, the shape of their image of the universe.
The voice told me that entire generations had been harnessed
to the task, families and clans, and vast holdings of wealth been
sacrificed to the delirious vision of a world of artificial caves;
young and old, rich and poor pouring out their lives, digging
in the dark. The construction was central to a belief system
that turned around the necessity for the invisible to reflect the
visible, an elaborate scheme concerning the tensile strength of
reality itself. If they failed to create a world that was invisible,
but that still literally was, the visible world would dissipate.
And they defined invisible as what is hidden from the light,
what the eye cannot perceive. So, vast populations were sen-
tenced to a subterranean labor, the carving out of a cosmos that
could never be seen, and that was – literally – hollow. In a long,
hushed aside, the voice began to explain the mechanics of the
thing, the crazy conviction, the dizzy mathematics that made it
all possible; but it was pushed aside by another voice, another
speaker's account of a woman who loved the sea and nightly
immersed her head in order to sing to it.

I remember too, the fantastic narrative of a library – a vast
glittering structure of books, of writing, measureless and beyond counting. Thousands of millions of books, the accumula-
tion of the art and knowledge of an almost equally uncount-
able number of civilizations. Histories and epics. Treatises and
novels. Herbaria and plays. Medical handbooks and bestiaries.
Poems. Biographies. Epistemological renderings. Thousands
of books of laws. Genealogies. Recipes. Instruction manuals
and legislation. And more. So very, very much more. All of it
housed in architecture composed on rigidly binaristic princi-
ples. A whole snaking, labyrinthine form built on a system of
simple "yeses" and "noes," blacks and whites, ones and zeroes.
Turn here and open an army of volumes on the history of battles under a particularly bloodthirsty dynasty of kings. Say "no"

and have a door open onto an orgiastic room whose shelves heave with breathless erotic poetry. Push a black door and find a ten-kilometer shelf of titles on the feeding and mating habits of birds. Turn the knob on the white and read forever on the case law of a culture too attached to capital punishment. One way there is only delight, turn another corner and the horrors lay slumbering, waiting for new discoverers. An almost infinite library, endlessly capacious, absolutely informative. Tumults of text vibratingly present waiting to be read. Indeed, not even waiting because one text leads to another, is intimately tied to every other title in the library. The reader who opens one cover makes sentences quiver in rooms far, far removed, on the far side of this library world, this labyrinth of words. One might start reading the life story of one's grandfather and finish in a Buddhist poet's images of hell. There is no definitive division between one tale and the next, between the Petrarchean sonnet in one's hands and the equation solved a generation ago, in another country, in another language. Simply rooms and spaces and shelves and pages and pages and pages. And one never has to go to the books, the voice told me, with a kind pleasure almost audible in it, because the words, the books, the heavy shelves were in themselves the world, surrounded you all the time while were you seated in your chair. And there was more mixed with it.

This you've forgotten. The thing you should most recall; generations of people enslaved to narrations. The myths that formed their cities and their wars. The lies of the powerful forcing their ways into homes, public squares, their very dreams. Freedoms that are not. Rhetoric able to turn black to white, war to peace, grinding poverty to the simple circulation of wealth. Here is a man whose voice seduces, false-hardy and with a surface of poor syntax. Listen to it sweeten and cajole, gentle distractions made of impossible promises, the jaws of sharks less cruel than all his warmth. Rose words and punctuation as sensual on the tongue as cactus fruit. Rivers of lost potential. Walls of possibilities.

Ignore them. I awoke from that account to find myself, and a half-dozen of my friends and collaborators in a dining room. A rope was in my hands, and in the hands of a few of them, and we were tying nooses. One rough rope was already hung, the great open coil of it waiting for a willing neck. A quivering sign hanging in the air. The still-entranced had busy hands, weaving more to join with it. We were all preparing our own deaths.

André was blanched. The shadow of the hanging rope a dark stain on his face. We had gone too far for him. And though he would never tell me in any detail what I had said that night, or how the group of us ended in that room, ended at our grim tasks, he slowed the pace of our seances. But even without André's report, I knew at least some of what I'd heard. Shortly thereafter he would stop the sessions altogether.

I knew part of his decision lay in fear: a new feeling for him. I also believe he was ready to end them, because he had learned what he could.

Oh, but there is more we can tell you. More world than that. More you can learn. Other worlds: a world of boiling water, its banks held aloft by the heated air and steam, hovering above everything, a world of loquacious cats, and one of cemeteries, its inhabitants erecting tiny, imperfectly functional residences among the massive monuments to their dead. A labyrinthine university. A speeding dorimitory on a trestle hurries towards you.

I'm sure there is, but I have little time left, and other things to do.

André was done with the sessions. For the last weeks he constantly took notes during them; writing in that elegant little book he carried everywhere. His face firm, his eyes bright. André's powers of concentration were vast. So intense was his expression, I thought I saw it radiate. It was foolish, I admit, but despite that naiveté I was sure where André fixed his archangelic glance, he could burn away darkness. And though the evidence seems grim right now, one can still hope that it is true.

When the period of sleeps finally came to end, I had the first of my bouts with illness. I spent a long time in bed recuperating. I spent the weeks reading and writing. Trying my hand at a couple of longer pieces, seeing where they led me. Testing the waters. I saw few of my friends, unable to join them in the chatter-filled evenings in cafes, the long, aimless afternoons drifting through dark movie houses. But André came to visit me a couple of times. I was startled by his solicitousness, and pleased.

The first visit we talked for an hour or so, about the trances and events around them. The disturbing eruption of coincidences that accompanied our nightly visions fascinated both he and I, but I said nothing of my secret narrations. André shared his fears about the aimlessness he saw in our companions, told me how much he felt the need for a new direction, a reinvigorating program for our generation of writers and artists, a great shared passion that might shape the course of things. Then we talked a bit about a woman he'd seen on the street and the curious sensation he felt of knowing her from somewhere else. It felt to me like he was changing the subject, but one never knew with André...he was constantly investigating the movement of his own mind; he could have been perfectly sincere in the sudden shift.

On his next visit, he was elated; he entered smiling and seated himself on my bed, took my hand in his and told me he wanted to share something special with me. I couldn't meet his gaze. He pulled some sheets from his pocket. The paper crinkled as he unfolded it. The sharp little sounds reminded me of the snaps and crackles of a fire as it gets going. Memory has its own ironies.

He began to read to me. As he did – impassioned but still firm – I knew by the slant of his forehead, the blaze that seemed to shine from it, that he cared past all reason about what he was reading. My hand burned where he had held it. A kind of flame whose progress I couldn't determine; was something tunneling to the surface from deep inside me, or was some invisible fire making its way towards my heart.

André read from the sheets steadily ignoring how they shook in his grasp. He spoke about the mind's terrible freedom, the infinite elasticity of language, its capacity to create vivid new images, scarcely conceivable new ways of thinking and being. He spoke of an infinite power of desire that ran through the word, through the heart, through the world.

His voice rose and fell with a strong, bodily rhythm, but never faltered, never shook. Never failed.

He spoke of a secret place in the mind where all the spirit's tensions stopped their antagonisms and light and dark, fire and ice, love and revolution fell together fornicating, and I could see a planet rise above a golden sea just past his left shoulder, a flight of giant birds with wings like mist lift from the rippling water as the mast of a sunken ship broke surface where they had been resting. Coming back, over and over again, to this place, this secret place in the mind, this absolute point of sure stillness where everything made sense and every possible contradiction was resolved. Where the shape of things, whole armies of meaning, was made clear. It shook me; how it shook me. But we did not linger at that edge.

André read on, speaking of tumult in the street, acts of random violence flowering in the desperate need for some space to feel free. A storm rose in his throat. Dreams and desire and death rolling over in a rushing stream, careless of the rocks where they lay.

He turned the page and chanted a litany of the names of our friends, and he aggrandized shamelessly their still small accomplishments.

Then I heard my own name, spoken as a devotee of the absolute limit. I saw a flicker of feeling on André's handsome face; he didn't pause, but he had clearly smiled at my sudden appearance in his text. He went on, the awesome golden vision in his voice more compelling by far than any offered me by my disembodied interlocutors.

My friend was in the grip of a presumption, he was planning the future, outlining a program of new possibilities for life and literature and love. It was an appalling hubris that he brandished so shamelessly, but it was beautiful. There was hope held out in those vertiginous words. There was something…something slight that vibrated in the tiny room we shared…but something nonetheless that one might finally believe in. Something worth an effort, worth committing to. My breath grew ragged as he read on.

And then he stopped. There was a silence. I was flushed and uncomfortable and unable to speak. And I realized then, panting a little, that under the blankets, as I lay listening, my cock had hardened. I was erect with the excitement those fabulous words had inspired in me.

I raised my knee to hide my response. It shook like a child's. My body temperature was spiraling out of control. What could I possibly say to my friend about this? I had no answer for this.

Happily André was too consumed with his text to notice my erection, but he did remark on my silence.

"Well," he asked.

"I am overwhelmed," I answered him. "Utterly overwhelmed." It was an understatement. In a half-hour of listening, André had bound me to the path I'd begun forever.

And his smile returned.

He told me he'd spent the last weeks pondering the group's experiments with trance, automatic writing and our countless enigmatic parlor games. How he felt the need to make some sense of it all, to trace their connections and measure the impact they had had among us. The rewards we'd found and the many risks we had stumbled upon as well. This last thing he said with a long, serious look.

For a moment I thought to ask him about what had actually happened to us on the night of the near-hangings, but I thought better of it. I crossed my legs and arranged my blankets, instead. My erection was lessening very slowly.

We talked a bit more. It was good and friendly and he embraced me before he left. In less than a year's time I would read some of those passages in my friend's pyrotechnical Manifesto.

But we would never again repeat those experiments; would never again fall into the delirious waves of trance. Or rather, we would never do so as a group again. I can't say as much for myself, because my voices and their multitude of stories never left me. Their speech went on.

BODIES
OF DESIRE

Though it goes without saying, I will make it clear: my feelings for André did contain some form of love or desire. He was a very handsome man, and a very charismatic one. His energy rushed over you and lingered at the same time. It was like standing in sunshine. A very hot sunshine. Yes, there was eros in my attraction to him and, I stress this, *his ideas*, but it was an unusual kind, and never, under any circumstances, did I act on it. I never wanted to. This desire, and the word is a poor placeholder for a feeling for which I have yet to discover a suitable substitute, was not *that kind* of desire. It wasn't as focused as the word usually implies. It was different. And I can assure you; I know something about different kinds of desire.

I had my first lesson in that the very first time I acted on desire's promptings.

It was the summer of my leave, the same beach in Normandy, the same girl who took me to her home and introduced me to Mme. Dante – the same day of the same meeting. The morning after the vanishing bird. That bright, windy morning.

I met the girl and we talked; that much you already know. We talked about small things at first, which felt right next to the vastness of the ocean and the sky: they were appropriately modest. In no time, we moved on to our unexpected confidences, the secrets we traded without calculation, without the tremor in the spine we feel whenever we open our hearts as adults. I remember no nervousness. I remember the light shining off her hair, making an iridescent nimbus of the down on her forearms. She had the finest lines at the corner of her mouth; they would crinkle and deepen slightly when she laughed. Because she was filled with delight, I imagined that she had earned them from an excess of laughter. And, for an hour in the brightness of the sun, her delight overflowed and filled me too.

We took off our shoes, walked barefoot along that broken line where sea met sand in a glittering rush while just beyond and to our right the trees of the orchards and the thick, green forest – another unknown, vast in its own way as the sea –

looked up at the indifferent clouds. As we rounded a point, she ran ahead, spun around and around on her axis, hair turning and billowing. In the coastal light it was a great honey-colored sail, full in the breeze, pulling some unseen ship to a new land. All at once she stopped; she scrambled up the beach towards the tall grass, the trees.

I heard her laugh again, a bright musical sound with a touch of brass in it.

She ran back towards me, still smiling, with her hands filled with flowers, vividly scarlet, red as a wound against the fairness of her skin. She tossed them at me, a rain of blossoms, and threw herself down against the sand. She tore open her light, pale blouse baring herself to me, and to the sun.

"Cover me with flowers," she cried out. "Crush them between my breasts."

The soft, round flesh gleamed whitely in the sunlight. Burned in my eyes.

I did. I pressed the red flowers between the nacreous white of her breasts. The perfume was overwhelming, pungent, sweet beyond describing.

Sweet. A sweet smell. A presence, somewhat hesitant, somewhat heavy in the air, but inescapable. So unlike the gas that has begun to fill my apartment now. It has no odour at all, just a continuous whisper that makes enormous promises whose implications I don't understand.

Strange that my desire should start with perfume, and end with its absence. Having loved passion so much in my life, surely it should have grown more fragrant by its end, or at least more pungent to me? Still, that is not my point; I have no interest in explaining my decision. Right now, this story is more important; I want to outline not my end, but the journey that brought me to it, and, after such a first experience of desire, my unique feelings for André held no fear or hesitation for me. They seemed right, exactly as they were.

*The whispers you spoke of, were they like us. Do they bring
you as much?*

My invisible interlocutors are back.

*We too can make promises. We have. Why will you not write
them down? Why will you not show the world all the miracles
that await it?*

Because they are not miracles. They are horrors. I can feel
them pull back a little.

No, they say. And, *No,* again. At least they do not insist so
much as they used to, but they never truly leave me now. Ignoring my attempts to cut them off, they rush on, having much to
say.

I never saw the girl after that summer, my season of spirit
visitations and beds of flowers. But it was my first passion. And
I would come to see many more of desire's curious faces, faces
with lingering glances, that turned their head away or fixed me
in the eyes with shivering determination. I would see them
over and over again beginning with my return to Paris. They
would start fast on the heels of the trances that greeted me.
That swept across my friends. Sex and seances making a curious pair. Terrible treasures.

Like these lovely things, these seashells, collected on that
beach the afternoon before I left to return to Paris and the barracks. Or this scaly foot, caught forever in its weakest state, all
the potential of its future ferocity trapped. When he gave it to
me, P. told me that the creature from which it was taken grows
to a terrible size and is a ferocious killer. He described it with a
great laugh as the closest thing in the world to an actual dragon.
That thought pleased him. It did me, as well. We are all of us
after a myth, I think. Every one of us scribbling our weird tales,
or drawing incongruous pictures, hopes for something that is
both vital enough and subtle enough to walk away from us and
into the lives of multitudes. Something that might actually live
intensely, truly. But this little foot isn't it. I put it down. All of its
predations are left undone. Nor is this box containing a touch

of opium, the last of my cocaine, however much pleasure I have found in them. Those too failed me. Like so much, Still, I could have a sniff while I wait for the darkness to arrive.

Or this, my skull-faced coffin nail. What of it? Why do I hold on to it? I've been torn apart by disease for most of my adult life; what perversity binds me to the awful image? If I wiped the dust from the mirror, how much might my face resemble it? Shit…. Once my face opened doors for me, the golden curls, the full lips, the sad boyishness. In the last years though, illness, the late nights, the drugs, have extracted a price. The hollow in the cheeks, the shadows under the eyes. My teeth. Not ruined, but certainly worn. Life pays what it must to death for just a little more pleasure, just a shade more time.

If I opened the window now, the gas would disperse and my rooms fill with dead leaves driven before the breeze. Not with red flowers. So why bother?

Let's leave Death for now and return to love and lust. Once one opens the door to desire, it enters; it takes a seat and makes itself at home. It never leaves, a kind of insistent, hungry and only occasionally humorous guest that doesn't worry himself overmuch about his welcome.

Some time after my encounter with the girl, I met my first real love, a handsome American named Eugene. I met him at the Ile St. Louis home of a British woman, an heiress with a weakness for rigorously fitted gowns, lavish entertaining and the company of artists and writers. She had a great wit and long, pale arms that were hung with ivory bracelets. She rattled with every movement. She rattled as she took Eugene's hand to introduce him to me.

Eugene was a painter, though it was never clear to me when he got his painting done. He poured so much of his time, his energy, even his *vision* into life. Few people I've met chased pleasure and sensation like Eugene. When I met him, I was struck by the strange combination of innocence and decadence that marked his behavior, a crazy hunger for experience that was ut-

terly indifferent to kind or consequences. A rushed encounter
with a sailor in a public toilet was as transcendent as dinner
at the *Tour d'Argent* or a Brahms requiem. He loved strength
and sensuality equally; he made no distinction between them
and with a breathtaking passion he wanted to both please and
overwhelm. He was a legion of contradictions and another of
delights. Even the group around André, who would begin to
call themselves "Surrealists" around this time, was less violently
committed to testing the limits of experience than he.

Eugene dazzled me. He dazzled me the way light can. He
was golden, blonde, fair-skinned (as the flower girl was), white
of tooth. He almost shone; but unlike André, he didn't shine
like the sun. Eugene's light was more electric: sharp and, in
some ways, artificial. And he struck me – as light does – in the
eyes first. Later I would notice what a large shadow he cast.
But not at first. Not in the beginning. Not when the first touch
of Eugene's lips, a sudden unexpected kiss as I tried to make a
phone call from that wealthy woman's study, drove all doubt
from me. His mouth touched mine, his trim hips and sculptur-
al shoulders, shattering contact, pushed me into a new world.
One that turned on an axis of his company.

We would charge out nightly from those sumptuous rooms
on the Ile St. Louis – appropriated, with the heiress' quiet con-
sent, as a base of operations. Clockwork sorties, fierce quests
for pleasure, for bright lights, for shrill laughter, for wine and
other intoxicants, for every drop and flavor of sensation. The
three of us went everywhere, N., our heiress, Eugene and I.
All of Paris' bold-faced names greeted us. Chic restaurants
and smart homes threw open their doors. His charm and her
wealth were perpetually renewable invitations to soirees as lus-
trous as N.'s pearls. We dined with Duchesses and Senators;
once, I recall, there was an evening in the home of a Viscount
at which we watched films in a private screening room while
servants poured drinks and rolled little balls of opium for our

pleasure. On another evening we toasted a millionaire's engagement on a boat in the river.

At that time I favored brightly colored shirts and ties, hues that made me giggle but raised eyebrows in the homes of our wealthier, well-connected friends. On other evenings, they attracted no attention whatsoever. Those were the nights we hurried to the clubs and bordellos. There, my extravagances seemed innocuous. We would dare every dive, see every show, every new *artiste* with a veil to shake, a fan to flash, and would lend their sequins greater brilliance with occasional jolts of cocaine. We heard jazz freshly imported from America, saw an Amazonian woman walk the length of a bar in a nearly transparent costume. In one sordid basement, girls disguised, as angels on one side and demons on the other, enacted a tug of war until one team was pulled into a vat of some viscous custard.

Deep, deep in the night, we made our way to the gay clubs and the challenging laughter of their painted entertainers and equally costumed patrons. My first glimpse of that world is seared into me. I was thrilled and shocked: it was all so new, so startling…. I reel thinking about how long it took me to come to it. My first sights, first sounds: a rouged young man in the arms of soldier, thighs pressed together, their hands shameless. One of the capital's brightest literary stars, safe from prying eyes in this demimondaine half-light, cackling with his coven of effeminates, the walls of gender collapsing before the hurricane of their humor.

It was so glamorous and so frightening. I broiled with contempt and swelled with all the secret pride of an initiate. No one "respectable" knew of this, but I did.

And every evening ended with the most pointed pleasure of all; just before the sun finally blushed at the ruins of our excess, Eugene and I would fall into bed together and my cock would swell under his masterful ministrations. How I came to love those dawns and hate the afternoons that followed, when I would awake with my head throbbing and my heart sunk at what I could remember: the tinny gales of titters and guffaws, the easy intimacies, the superficial conversation and false compliments, the glimpses – uncommented on – of Eugene's hand too high on the thigh of our waiter or some nightclub boy whose nimble dancing had "captivated" us an hour before. So many glib exchanges, so much chattering. In the cooling light of the mid-afternoon I would recoil from those images and nurse my head over three, four, five cups of coffee, preparing myself to squeeze a day's writing into a few hours in order to be ready to do it all over again that night.

All in the eager anticipation of the fall into bed at the end of it all. His strong touch on my waist, the warm miracle of his mouth as he took my cock in, sliding on it. His kiss. The gold cloud of light that seemed to surround us like a veil in the high, narrow room. The flurry of feelings heightened by the alcohol, the drugs, our hunger for one another. That hour that seemed to unfold forever like a spool of glittering, golden thread, or the speckled skin of an interminable viper.

We kept on this way for months. Not every night, but many. Too many. Pleasures like these are fiery wheels: they turn in circles and they always burn. The burning and spinning had to stop.

It did. I fell ill again: a collapse of the lungs that left me gasping and fearful. Though not wholly caused by them, my nocturnal excesses undoubtedly exacerbated it. And faced with no meaningful choice, I decided to take some time away from my pleasure-chasing friends. And some space.

My disease took me to the mountains, the highest mountains I could find. My illness needed clean air, and I wanted the feeling of remoteness, and of savagery. I wanted something natural. I chased a different kind of pleasure: one less physically taxing and more restorative, one less corrupted by the jealousy that even in the midst of our debauches stirred in me, a small creature armed with pins that lived unseen in my entrails, but that stirred every time Eugene whispered in another ear, took too long bringing back drinks, vanished for an unseemly time in the men's room. Stirred and stuck me with sharp little jolts, stings when they were least welcome. No it had to stop. I had to freeze that wheel.

In the high mountains the air shimmered with light unrelated to that of Paris, that of Eugene. I was alone. I was *removed*, far away from all the business of my life and able to see its detail as if miniaturized, made manageable by the height. From there I could, in my imagination, see the tiny figures of men and women whipping through a labyrinth of miniaturized buildings. There a thimble-sized couple – minuscule man, diminutive woman – quit a tiny bar, shouting at each other in a tone as slight as the thrum of a dragonfly's wings. Here, a car the size of a half-used bar of soap pulls up at a negligible corner, teacup sized and empty. Department stores as broad as my two hands spread on a table top, appeared, swallowing up waves of almost substanceless shoppers. A Seine like a grey grosgrain ribbon wound through my mental landscape. And all of this activity was speeded up, shrunken down through the power of perspective. Everything I had spent my evenings doing rendered small and slightly ridiculous. I pulled back, when I heard my invisible narrators return with new stories of that toy city's impalpable counterparts. So much imagining encouraged them, I told myself, but I knew that at least part of my caution was a desire to not look too closely at anything while I felt so weak.

Instead, I spent my time differently. My days were slow and clear. I walked in the Alpine meadows and listened to the quiet. I dined alone. I read, devouring Dostoyevsky and marveled at what writing could do. What power might it have if a single book could go that far? I slept a great deal, as well, pampering my lungs, begging them to inflate, nourishing my failed energy.

I corrected the proofs for a new book of my own and I wrote letters. Letters that organized my thoughts, made sense of my experience, either outlining all that tumult for a friend, or –

with other parts of my past – shutting it down, cordoning it off with ambiguity and half-explanation in an attempt to foreclose any "loving" censure.

And I wondered, I think, is the right word. I wondered at the violence of peaks: sharp, white, stony heights. The mountaintops, where colors bleed away, and the air thins to its purest essence. When I began to feel stronger, I walked on the slopes and took in the rocks and the broken, skeletal trees with wide eyes and rapid pulse. I would walk the mountains until walking became climbing. Often, I took myself as far up as I could without a mountaineer's special equipment. Sometimes, when the temperature rose, I would shed all of my clothing and walk naked, enjoying the warmth and the touch of sun on skin. Sadly, my dreams of bawdy shepherds were never actualized, though on one or two occasions I did provoke scandal among some visiting English tourists. Bright, brisk mornings and sunny afternoons alike, I pulled myself over rocks and logs, forced through the last of the brush, jumped back from the sudden drops, always casting nervous looks towards the village and my small hotel. Whether from nostalgia or contempt, I can't tell you.

One day I went out for my ramble on the mountain a little later than usual. I made my way along a familiar path. The day was good; a strong sun, a temperature that was bracing enough, but still very comfortable. I made my way up, thinking about my work and my friends, about the intensities of the surrealists, and my handsome, faithless lover. So many threads already tangled my story; what would it look like at fifty? I came upon an open patch of grass, green fading under the low clouds, I crossed a line of animal tracks pressed into the soil, parallel rows of hoof prints, deep enough to suggest the beast that made them was large and heavy. Probably horned; cattle, or a ram perhaps. I stepped across the line. I moved further up the mountainside. It grew steep, and my breath came heavier. I lay down to give my lungs a little rest. The ground was cool, the grass rough on my back. I shut my eyes and waited. Nothing came to fill my mind; time vanished in a resonant blackness.

When I opened my eyes again, the sun was low in the sky. Exhausted, I had slept hours and the day was ending. I jumped up, wanting to be down off the mountain before darkness fell. Knowing it was impossible. I moved faster than I had on my ascent, desperate to be home before night made the paths unsafe. The shadows thickened as I went down, the light fell off the cool grey rocks. Darker and darker. Still I hurried. Details vanished, gloom thickened and spread. Soon, it was so dark I could hardly see my hand when I held it up, and I was still high on the slope, far from my warm room. But I kept moving, begging my memory, hoping it could guide me down. No moon was overhead as I pushed through the night. Stepping as fast as I dared to, as slow as I had to, I stumbled against rocks and dead branches and unexpected irregularities in the ground. A wind came up. The air cooled. One side of my brain shouted stubbornly at the other, insisting we could find our way back. The other half slumped silently: surrendered. The sounds coming off the peak were deep, resounding, ending in a grumble and a trill. I was lost. The angry half of my brain shouted the thought out. I wanted to run, but I stopped moving. I stopped where something told me – a scent on the breeze, a change in the feel of the ground beneath me – that a precipice waited, the edge of a high cliff. I stood there while the drop lay just before me. I waited before that terrible fall in that terrible darkness: an ocean of night. Dark, dark, dark.

The black sky, untroubled by a handful of distant stars, and the black of open air just past the mountain's edge were indistinguishable; it was all one vast, continuous void. I leaned into a sea of tar whose bubbles simmered atop it but never burst. They just sank back beneath the surface. There, at the world's edge, things melted into one another, lost their separateness. They went dark and seamless and still. And they didn't go at all. They stopped, swallowed in shadow. One of my voices suddenly stirred, telling me how a day might come when there would be no more darkness, humanity would light up the whole world as it has done already to the great boulevards. I shoved the voice away from me, too enamored of the naked dark. The voice fell back into the deep, shouting as it descended, tales of a city that blinded a third of its children in order to seal them in a windowless tower where they kept the royal chronicles, trained to write by a rigorous physical training of their hand and still unable to read the dynastic secrets they recorded.

It was I. It was I who told you that tale and there is more. On the morning of the Spring Equinox, the chronicles are brought out and into a public square.

I don't care, nor did I then.

This is it; I told myself, this is – at last – an absolute. I shook, head to toe, with a triumphant despair, a great burning enthusiasm that consumed anything I might call my character, my "me," and left only some naked, inhuman exhilaration. Here, I wanted to shout, everything falls into darkness. An absolute darkness. At last, an absolute. I remembered the rush of words André had unfolded for me in my hospital bed: his certainty that we could find just this, such magic. Now, I knew he was right; we could find that unconditional place. We find it – the unqualified, the continuous and infinite – at the furthest edge, the limits of things. I knew all at once: this is what the thin air and the raw breeze and the final, limitless dark had to tell me. We find the absolute only at the end. And, we find it in the end itself, in danger and death and darkness. In motionlessness and quiet. In the indescribable and the contentless. In change, silent or violent. In transformation. At the end, the very end of things, of life, of language. At the limit is the truth.

I was ready to throw myself into this knowledge, to hurl myself into that dark sea. I was ready to jump. I took a step forward, knowing, or almost knowing, that solid ground ended there. That I would fall, and fall, and fall in open, hungry darkness. And just then, a shower of shooting stars flew by in the heavens. Brief, bright movement and I felt my heart stop in my chest for a second. An infinitesimal series of flashes that went out as soon as they began. They were beautiful and scarcely significant in the great black void in which they – happily – spent themselves. They were there, mired in it, and they burned and vanished. They vanished perfectly.

And I learned that I couldn't, not yet. I turned around. I turned my back on it. I would go back down the mountain. I too must burn in the dark before I went out.

It took me almost all night, but I made it down. I found the path, just barely. I thought of nothing but what I had heard in the dark. I thought of nothing but the hidden end of things. I returned to Paris not long afterwards, a man broken by illness and recovery, but remade by the limitless. I missed my friends and was eager to see them again, and eager to know if the changes in me were perceptible; if they would detect them.

In a pleasing inversion, I felt dizzy when I came back to the city; my head swam at the lights and the long, smooth Hausmannian facades with their implacable composure. The grey trees seemed to cling to the sidewalks on the boulevards as if they felt themselves about to lift off and float into the sky and wanted a last embrace. The odors rising from the open mouths of metro stations were pungent, the fragrance of alchemical experiments. Everything churned when measured against the quiet boundlessness of the mountains. Everything seemed fraught with conflict and with change.

And all of it seemed wonderful to me. Happy uncertainty. Happy change. A sweet satisfaction because I knew that the absolute waited at the end. A gorgeous black backdrop against which all the colors flamed. The kiss from Eugene that greeted me spun through that dark fire.

I spent a few days settling back in, reconnecting with my friends; though my romance with Eugene was sputtering out, we would still swan through bars and restaurants with regularity. Given that my book was more or less complete after my stay in the Alps there was book business to deal with as well, and the almost daily attendance of surrealist gatherings at our favored cafés. André put great stock in these, and his control over the group was growing more and more total. The meetings were lively, filled with talk and ideas and plans. They grew more frequent and more passionate as we began to publish a new magazine as well, which, in its turn, began to attract more and more attention to our activities and us.

The magazine was filled with the records of our dreams, reported in detail, with scientific objectivity and no comment, mirroring and mocking learned journals. They were accompanied by visionary automatic texts generated as we sat for hours in cafés or stayed up too late in our apartments. Photos of mundane neon signs above shoemakers' shops, or milliners, or hand-scrawled notices in the windows of pawnshops littered the pages. There were more and more vehement political treatises decrying our era's rush to cretinization. Verbal assaults on piety and patriotism. Affirmations of our solidarity with the poor and dispossessed, or with the criminal classes, against the smug, comfortable men in power appeared. We flirted more and more with revolution, and we wrote endless poems. There were reports and surveys too, one about suicide that provoked great response from the group. My friends were surprised by the vehemence of my affirmations on this point. Though I could have responded to their questions, I didn't. I knew how close I had come to a single, transcendent act of self-negation and been remade by it; I felt freed. There's no way to explain that.

And there was even more café debate than before: we poured over questions of a political nature, and dissected people's experiences of the streets at odd times of the day. We talked about fantasies, which fascinated me as they gave me a window into the thoughts and attitudes of my colleagues. I saw André's too, to my great consternation and discomfort; he had an irrational hatred of homosexuality and when he spoke of it, it was in the most poisonous of terms. I said nothing, but wondered what he might think of the way I spent some of my evenings. Many surrealists were less hateful; many scarcely gave the matter of men's desire for other men a thought. Some I had seen in the bars and clubs Eugene and I frequented, so their silence or acquiescence had another significance for me.

One night around this period, I picked my friend J. up at his apartment for an evening out. I say friend, though our relationship was often strained. Still, we did spend some time together, so I'll let the word stand. André hated him; he loathed his glib tongue, the fashionable success his books and plays enjoyed among Paris' aesthetically inclined *rentiers*, and most of all he hated him for the openness he showed concerning his love of men. This was a brew that was guaranteed to turn André's stomach. He savaged J. at gallery openings, at readings and film premieres, in print too. For a while, a woman with whom he was having a particularly turbulent affair lived in the same building as J.. The encounter was inevitable. And it was as ugly as I feared.

J. and I were descending the staircase; he was dressed dapperly, as always, and I was in one of my garish, brightly colored ensembles. Kelly green shirt with a violet tie, if memory serves. We were laughing as we headed out, joking with one another about shared friends and the scene and the minor scandals that rocked it and were, by and large, invisible to most of the world.

A floor or two below us, I saw André ascending, taking the steps quickly. I could tell by his gait he was unaware of anyone else on the staircase. My laughter froze – sharp, cold bits of ice, slicing to ribbons the joke that had been on my lips a second before. In an instant our paths crossed; a momentary flash of warmth, or recognition played across his face as he saw me. And vanished as he saw J. He turned to stone. Cold and stiff, he climbed each step mechanically, and when he was face to face with us, he glared at my companion, said "Good evening, Madame," and passed by. He didn't even acknowledge my presence. J. stopped in his tracks. He said nothing. I saw the slightest movement in his shoulders as if he might turn around; follow his insulter up the stairs. He shook his head and continued the descent. Neither or us spoke a word until we were outside and a block from the building.

My heart pounded the next day as the hour approached for all good surrealists to gather at the Cyrano, our new café, for our near-daily meeting. I paraded a whole carnival of scenarios through my mind: André greeting me with a poisonous re-mark, the conclave of my friends and partners in an intellectual adventure I loved more than anything all turning their back on me as I entered the smoky room, a tract denouncing me read to the assembled group. I changed my mind a half-dozen times about whether or not to attend that night.

Finally, I decided it was better to know my fate at once, and face it bravely.

I actually pulled back my shoulders at the bar's front door; I feel ridiculous describing it, a melodramatic gesture from some sort of train-station novel. But it's the truth. And the action, even as I made it, felt, to me, self-conscious and cold-blooded.

I walked into the café squared off and jaw up. A few of the surrealist crowd dominating the back of the room turned when they sensed my approach. Their eyes were blank as they ran over me. It was unbearable. I was waiting for some sign as I walked towards them.

André interrupted what seemed like a lively conversation with a young woman to his left. His head came up, acknowl-edging my arrival. His expression changed. Was it cruel? Iron-ic? Perhaps even sincere? It flickered across his face for aeons: a glacier could have spread across the hemisphere in the time it took his teeth to show in a smile, an age of reptiles could have passed from the world.

"Ah, René!" he called out at last, "you've arrived. It feels like an age since we last talked. Sit. Sit here. We need your opinion on the next issue."

And it was done. No comment at all on our stairway encounter. André was willing, it seemed, to turn a blind eye to my tastes. There was, of course, no possibility he was unaware of my – let's merely call it, lively social life. I made no effort to hide anything, no polite gesture to discretion, since beginning my late night adventures. I saw no point in doing so; my life was my own and I only shared it with those who cared to take part. Still, despite my insouciance about some of his prejudices, I thought certainly, this time, the provocation of J.'s company, would have been too much. It appeared not to be the case; André seemed as friendly as ever.

So I sat, stress left my body only to be replaced by a leaden heaviness. My arms weighed me down, a pain twisted in my guts; I felt I would never understand André. Never know any real intimacy with him.

But the meeting went well. Articles were discussed. The games that were more and more central to us were played. In one we redefined colors: red, an infant born singing; black, a mirror that swallows images. And there were more. In another the group chased visions by constructing mysterious sentences through the addition of words and phrases to a folded piece of paper with no knowledge of what had been written before. At the end of the round, it was unfolded and we read out our haul of fantastical imagery. Weird narratives, microscopic tales of enchanted sewing machines, or serpentine women speaking oracles in Greek, and backwards. In one case the sentence spoke directly to my secret life: I flinched as it was read aloud, but no one could make the connections I imagined so bald-faced. The crazy phrase, however, helped me riddle my way out of a bad patch with Eugene.

However, most of that night's discussions turned around the overtures made to a group of militants in the organized left.

Such overtures were more and more common in those months as the radicalized Surrealists sought their way out of what they increasingly saw as the impasse of art and literature. We clawed and grasped at a way to make the society we lived in, and the way we lived our daily lives, as filled with shimmering marvels as our poems. That night, the heated arguments ran for hours and we decided to pursue the relationship with the militants; André even suggested I might be a good choice for the next discussion with them.

In fact, my initial trepidation aside, nothing untoward occurred at the meeting; André's affection was undiminished it seemed to me, and I enjoyed every hour of it. That is, until very near the end of the meeting. Then André said there was one more item to be discussed. He paused. Raised his chin and announced the matter of D., stating that he had compromised the intellectual rigor of the surrealist group by writing commercial journalism for the popular, and occasionally right wing press. There were murmurs around the table, some nodding of heads. I had heard news of a growing trend towards group discipline among my friends while I was recovering at the mountains; that evening I had my first actual experience of it. André slowly outlined how such work hurt the group's project, called us into disrepute, weakened our position and was an inexcusable collaboration with retrograde cultural and political forces. Someone shouted out his agreement. André began to weave a skein of arguments; each one more pointed than the one preceding it, as to why such behavior was unacceptable among members of the group. How it damaged – irreparably – our shared attempts to liberate the mind and transform experience, and how it could not be accepted. A whisper ran round the tables. He concluded by calling for discussion on the exclusion of D. from the surrealist group, and discussion broke out.

Members of the group declared their contempt for D.'s journalistic efforts, his inexcusable bourgeois connections, and his counter-revolutionary sympathies. They pointed to a whole ar-

ray of questionable past actions and ambiguous public state-
ments. Motionless in the storm of declamation, André sat stol-
id-faced, looking into his glass from time to time. The debate,
if that's what it was, ran for over an hour and at the end of it
André called for a vote on the accused's exclusion. It passed
unanimously. In the space of an evening D. was driven from a
community that had been central to his life, that had nurtured
his writing and opened up a world of ideas and visions that
he might never have encountered before. I knew that it was
ruin for D. There was not one of these men and women who
would speak to him again. For him, a great voyage was done,
and André had brought it to pass without a trace of sentiment.
I choked at the thought of how easily it might have been me,
given our staircase encounter last night.

To understand the impact of this you have to understand
that the force of André Breton's personality is so vast that it's
physical. His attention, his friendship warms you, brings your
ideas, your dreams and projects to flower and to fruit. André is
solar, all light and heat and fire, but that night I saw the dark
side of that sun, how it could also scorch and burn and turn a
whole land into desert. I feared the loss of him as a child fears
the indissoluble horror of darkness. And though, of course, I
still enjoyed my dizzy nights, the sudden understanding that
I had avoided the loss of him flooded me with relief. I threw
myself into my writing and the work of the group with vigor
and became busier than ever.

Still, work is never enough to satisfy all one's needs. I wanted
more; more pleasure, more intensity, more of the light and more
of the darkness, more affirmation and more abandonment. I
wanted to feel the freedom and loss of self-consciousness, the
uncertainty I had found standing at the edge of the void in the
mountains. And Paris, being what is, can offer you anything,
even that. I heard about this opportunity in the unlikeliest of
places: in the giggles and gossip of my nocturnal excursions
with N. and Eugene.

Near the heart of the city is a park; it's a good size, thick with trees and bushes. The oaks and poplars are tall, leafy shrubs cling to their bases like children tugging at their mothers' hems eager to share some new discovery, and many of its paths and benches are all but invisible from the street. I've always imagined that from overhead, the straight, cobblestone paths must resemble a great, grey spider web, shimmering at the heart of Paris. Waiting for things to become trapped in it. And things do.

Because it is near the centers of business and trade, it's a noisy, animated place during the day. Workers and students and passing shoppers pause there for a moment of rest, a quarter-hour of idle, pleasant conversation. Sandwiches are eaten, boys run and shout. Young women trade confidences, and look for ways to escape their familial impositions. At either end, a fountain sparkles. All of this happens in a flurry of birds and the gleam of sunlight. Policemen pass by. Delivery boys. Bakers. Thieves. Civil servants, scuttling. The precise lecturers from the colleges across the river. Engineers and antiques dealers.

Then evening comes; the park grows quiet, shadows lengthen; they take on life and reach out for each other across the expanses of grass and cobbles, eager to touch after the long, bright hours of isolation. The crowd flees, its once-patrons crowding, instead, into bars and cafés and restaurants.

At last the pools of shadows on the lawn spread their bulk out; darkness takes over with all the ceremony of the house lights going down in a hushed theatre. Cool, resolved, anticipatory. The whole park becomes deliberate – the trees carefully placed, the shrubs tailored, the lawns clipped artfully, all of its formality and artifice is transformed into a set. The chestnuts, groomed into careful volumes, the tapered firs, are backdrops, fashioned to match nature's dimensions but too fine, too perfect to be real. The beds of flowers find their colors muted as if by design. The glow of the lamps become spotlights for the extraordinary performances to come.

A great outdoor theatre materializes in the dark and is witnessed only by the initiates that start to gather. They drift into the web of paths and copses from the smaller entrances, not the tall arched entranceways that face the twin fountains. They slide in from side streets, and culs-de-sac, and the small neglected squares that hide behind the elegant shops and colonnades. They take possession of the dark corners, the dimly lit aisles, soundlessly.

When one my acquaintances, on a noisy evening out, told me about this park, it was that silent procession that impressed him most. How dozens of men could drift into the space without a noise, without attracting attention. He was not wrong to comment on it; it is an extraordinary thing, but there are others more startling,

These gathering shadows take the waiting stage prepared for them. Their movements stiff, their entrances and exits unpredictable as if they were players in some esoteric school of shadow puppetry. Or, perhaps, the ancients' ceremonial plays in which masked figures gestured hieratically in the smoke and fire and sounding gongs. Except there is no noise. These men, in the deepest part of the night, perform something related to, though distant from, what unfolded at the Theatre of Dionysus. Both a play and a ritual. Ceremonies of hunger, of love, of need, of cruelty, and, at times, of terrible violence too.

Look, and see them, there.

There, among bushes, two men kiss each other, thick with appetite, their bodies comprised of verdure and shadow and the sound of leaves brushing against leaves. In the unequal light their faces slide into each other, sharing substance. Two brows, for an instant, frame a single eye, a pair of chins flutter against one another, become the broad, pale wings of a gigantic moth, and then, pulling back, are chins again. Their lips are swollen from frottage against late-night growths of beard, and wet with copious drool, crystalline in the faint light falling on them. Their erections bob, pale ships on a sea of darkness. The paired men break their hungry embrace; the fairer, younger of the two, glides to his knees, a courtier rendering graceful homage, adjusting the trousers around his ankles with impeccable precision and no noticeable effort. He takes the other man's cock in his mouth with devotion and with need. His head slides down its formidable length as a cloud passes over the moon.

Behind a nearby tree a man's broad, sun-browned hand can be seen squeezing a pale buttock. Dark, somewhat dirty, fingers are lines of paint on the porcelain ass. He turns his pale companion to his side, one ruddy hand rises to an invisible mouth, returns, two fingers wet with spit and slides between the cheeks. The rough thrusting is palpable. Determined. But the ass pushes back to meet it.

Night after night such mysteries are met in the abandoned park. Now and again I quit the heated debates of my friends and co-revolutionists, their furious hunt for dreams and miracles, to return here and find some. I come to watch and take my place in these…rehearsals of limitlessness.

One time, late, I saw a vast pulsating creature materialize on the darkened stage: a great, twisting protozoon. A cluster of men buggering with brilliant abandon. One behind another, some on their knees, in a tight, seamless circle of flesh that twisted and turned. Their individual distinctions vanished in the knot of shadowy trees, just the odd arm protruding from the pullulating mass only to be sucked back beneath the heaving, pink membrane of their shared skin. Dark patches of hair appeared like visionary animals in the morass of ass and arm and broad, heaving back.

There were times I saw spirits, glowing naked angels, slipping between trees, brazen, sublime, utterly free of shame. Semi-erect cocks slapping against their thighs made new music, until they vanished once again.

Once, far from any light, a drunken faun, clothes lost, bent against an oak and wordlessly offered me his ass. Before such grace, I was speechless and took it gratefully.

Every night, and long into the night, the men come to act out strange scripts, and to learn new ones. Countless ferocious copulations are undertaken with concentration, with so much commitment and deliberateness and sheer care that they cease being rut and are made artful. Performances worthy of the park's sublime structures, its architecture and elegance, devotions so beautifully performed that the clear-throated orisons of cathedrals everywhere might grow quiet before them. The bent knee both a theatrical gesture and a spiritual one. The men's wanton prostrations rise to allegory; a masque that might have been performed in the court of a forgotten anti-pope. The carved trees for props, the wide expanse of night a curtain. All of it artifice – monstrous and marvelous.

Once I made my way to the mysteries; I passed the pools of light surrounding the fountain and headed to the heart of it all, the stretch of park furthest from the streets. On this night the shadows seemed thicker than usual, more tangled, as if they too had lost themselves in lust. I made my way quickly, eager to be among the wonders. Out of the corner of my eye I saw a blinking red light; the end of cigarette flaring up, dying down again, a tiny spot of red and gold asserting itself in the ambient gloom. I stopped, trying to make out the shape behind the cigarette. Perversely curious, I turned towards it. A dark man of middle height was smoking. His eyes were deep set and his lips were full. He looked directly at me as I approached; his gaze never turned aside. That was unusual here, where boldness is always wedded to quiet and discretion. As I drew near, I could see the pallor of his cheekbones. Then I was beside him, and surprised at how quickly the shadows settled in around us. How dark the spot he had chosen to hide in actually was.

He said, "Do you want something?"

No one had ever asked me that before. Not here. I pulled back, involuntarily, surprised. I caught myself; grinned, thinking that was more appropriate. My hand went out to cup his crotch, as I had done so many times before. As so many had done to me. He was already hard. He tossed the cigarette aside. His hand ran up my belly, over my chest and to my neck. It never even touched my groin. The hand on my neck tightened slightly; my face grew warm as blood rushed there.

He spoke again. "I guess you do."

I brought my face in to kiss him. The hand on my throat released me and in a movement so fast it was undetectable it struck me lightly on the check. I was stunned and pulled back again. But made no move to leave. His smile now was broader. His hand came back to my face; rubbing against the place he had struck me only a second before.

"You do want something, don't you? Show me how badly." And he pushed me to my knees. And out of some place in my mind, darker by far than the dark green world around me, came a gnawing hunger that rose from the wells of my brainstem and flooded every nerve and synapse, every cell and tissue of me. I wanted this man more than anything I had ever longed for. I pulled his hard cock from his fly and swallowed it whole while waves of flame melted flesh and tissue and tongues of salty water made them whole again. My mouth filled with his taste, my face smoldered where his hand had been and I – I will never know why – ached for him to hit me once again and make the feel of his sex in my mouth more real and more immediate. I wanted him, all of him. I wanted to choke on him. His cock. The curve of his smile. The open, black pits of his eyes. The force of his hand. The impossible strength and boldness of the way he shoved me down. And filled with all this longing, I sucked and sucked at him as he pulled my head into the pleats of his trouser, scented with smoke, making me gag and choke. Leaving me happy to do so for him. Eager to give up breath for his pleasure. Aware of nothing but this man and his enjoyment of me.

It took minutes and I have held to the memory ever since. He came in my mouth, flooding me with his thick, salty taste. I swallowed every drop of it and almost sobbed like a child when he pulled his cock from my mouth.

I got to my feet; nearly falling over as my head spun and my heart snapped. He buttoned his pants back up, without so much as a glance at me. He turned to walk away. My hand came up, unconscious, as if to hold him back. I let it fall, embarrassed at the gesture. Then, he turned to me, smiling a small smile. He grabbed me by the back of the neck once more, tight. He pulled me close to him and kissed me, long and hard. His face flushed with heat. And he let me go.

He turned and walked away.

And all the while the voices of my disembodied companions churned in my head, egging me on in my blissful abjection. Telling me stories of a time and place where whole quarters of the city would be given over to this, a whole nation of people who joined together in endless fuckings in order to open doors and make themselves understood to each other because they had no words for individual identity.

And I asked myself: how many more sabbats of this kind were celebrated in the park. And my phantom voices answered – *how many more will be?* Unable to answer myself, I responded to them instead; it will go on forever.

No it will not. Not endure. Not reform. Not unfold unfalteringly. Your deep ceremonies go on a while, grow deeper and achieve a final flowering only to fall before their success. They scintillate an hour in the darkest sky. They shine with so much shadowy brilliance that the stages on which they built their secret pride can no more contain them than one sea can all the world's waters. They leave the hidden places to share pleasures with the crowd. A sudden burst, a flash of light and it is done; a hundred cities host a hundred halls where men share flesh and fire in a dark grown less absolute. Here are the names they conjure with, the names of beasts and weaponry, the borrowed devices of combat and of labor. A phalanx of clichés deployed without reserve on every street, an open invitation to delight.

They will be everywhere and much enjoyed. Until the flavor
fails and pleasure made too popular grows pale. In time the
only satisfaction to remain is that of being sought and all these
eager men will satisfy themselves with mere display. There.
Again. A grey room filled with tunnels made of glass. The naked prowl, stalk the softly lit processional – a light that flatters
everyone – until a gaze, some felt and some observed, compels
them to stop. They turn to offer nakedness and shake, as if
overcome by the bliss of an expanding pupil. No need to touch
at all, not now. The pleasure rests in being wanted; what else
might matter anyway. The bumping together of genitals is too
banal by far. And if a player's sense of protocol should falter,
well, the walls of glass protect the edifice of taste. They cannot
touch through that. Looking and feeling someone else's need is
lust enough for these.

I was unconvinced that night. I am less so now. Joined to
these ceremonies I had others to fill my time as well: surrealism, my writing, and my friendships. I would work on a new
book into the afternoon, then attend the daily meeting, or join
some of the group in a day-long walk through obscure neighborhoods or cemeteries or flea markets seeking out the one
building or the single object powerful enough to make us stop.
We were on the hunt, eager to discover the secrets buried in
what surrounded us. Behind every door a magical courtyard
awaited, in every abandoned book or hundred-year-old house-
hold implement the lineaments of paradise might be discerned.
Our whole life was adventure (how accurately we had named
that early magazine.) But the paradox of so much activity, of
course, is the way in which it engenders more activity.

So, my enthusiasm for new adventures led me to travel; new
friendships tempted me to Berlin. I was breathless with anticipation when I left Paris. And breathlessness would mark the
whole of my stay. The visit was stimulating, filled with new
connections, handsome strangers and the strained social and
political life of the German republic as it slid towards fascism,

but, what marked it most, in the dash between galleries and gay bars, between late night discussions and visits to artists' studios, was that my lungs failed me once again, and unequivocally this time. It was during my stay in Germany that my long-running respiratory troubles were definitively diagnosed as tuberculosis and I was obliged to take up residence in a clinic for treatment.

For months I rested and submitted to my doctors' attentions. First, the observation, and then the interventions: needles, lancings, at one point a surgery to deaden a nerve in the hopes the lung would inflate more easily. I lived with pain and boredom, but most of all I suffered under a treacherous hopefulness as one treatment showed promise and then failed, only to be replaced by another. To fill the hours, when my strength was high, I penned the introduction for the catalogue accompanying a painter's new exhibition. I received visits from friends as if my hospital room were a salon where we talked for hours. This way, I stayed abreast of the latest news and developments both in Berlin, and with my friends in Paris. News that was not always agreeable.

During my absence the surrealist group had organized a series of group debates on sexuality: long, intense detailed discussion of tastes and behaviors and interests. They ran over several sessions, were thorough, and involved frank discussion of individual tastes and practices. Unsurprisingly, the topic of homosexual activity came up. André condemned it rabidly, calling it a behavior so vile it was eschewed by animals. Though such idolized figures as de Sade received a magnanimous pass. Others were more accepting, sometimes indifferent, sometimes amused, but not disturbed or disgusted. André was outraged by such moral laxity…. In an unhappy mental image, I tried to conceive of how things might have gone had I been present in Paris for the meetings.

When, after a long, unpleasant recovery spent in the German clinic, I returned home, the atmosphere was taut. One night at the Cyrano, I popped in for a drink and spotted several surrealists at a table. As I came over to say hello, I heard one of them say something about the "sex talks" to another who rapidly glided over the question as I approached.

On another occasion I saw L. and P. pick up an old postcard in the flea market, a semi-nude woman from the end of the last century, skirts hiked up to reveal stockings and a pair of boots so laughably out of date that the whole image's foray into the erotic ended in laughter. P. laughed and said, "That is what I think you meant during the last chat." Nothing else was said, but the comment's enigma made it clear that I was missing information.

My friends couldn't possibly assume I was ignorant of the proceedings. I knew about the talks, and my friends knew I knew…but nothing was ever said about them, or the fact that my participation had not been requested, even by mail.

I found myself baffled by this marriage of eager talk and resolute silence, this circular gesture of not withholding, not providing. At the capacity of the whole group – under André's influence I was sure – to do contradictory things. It made no sense at all, until saw the issue of our magazine that dealt with the discussions. It was worse than I'd imagined. André had threatened to call the meetings to a close if the outrageous nonchalance about homosexual behavior continued. I put the issue on my bookshelf and swore never to look at it again.

I was furious with André. Raging at the incongruity of a man who had dedicated himself to the deepest imaginable exploration of the human spirit, the liberation of desire…the reconceiving of human life from top to bottom, but who couldn't come to grips with something as simple as a kind of love that was different from his own. It was unimaginable to me. It was made worse by knowing that despite his inflexibility, his narrowness, I loved him and cherished his friendship. A part of me needed it; needed his passion, his rigor, and his conviction, even his approval. I was angry with myself as well.

I poured a drink. And then another. And then another. Slumped into my chair and sat, doing nothing; counting my breaths. I took another issue of our magazine from my shelf, one older than this inflammatory survey. I read one of André's poems. In a handful of precise, delicate, beautiful lines he wrote of his longing, his quest, to love a woman always for the first time, over and over again. I read that five times before continuing. I cried. Other images rushed to join the line: white birds sheltering deep black eggs, the air of the water, a tower become a sunflower.

In tears, I remembered the day in my hospital room when he read to me, with so much passion in his voice that it quivered and broke with emotion, his hunger for some sacred place in the mind where all binaries ended, where the real and the imagined ceased their warring, where high and low, life and death were no longer in opposition. His most profound convictions, his deepest needs made him ready to hold a hundred different opinions and to love his contradictions. So he could love me even as he despised whole areas of my life. And in that instant, I knew that my friend, like me, was starving for the absolute, struggling for it…and I loved him, paradox of paradoxes, even more for holding me at arm's length. Knowing that it let him see me as he had to.

Then, putting down still another glass, one drink too many by far, I saw the moon over the great, grey dome of *Sacré Coeur* through my window and thought that so often it was changeable things that cast light. And I knew that my love for André, turbulence and all, was no failing on my part. It was inevitable.

BODIES
OF POWER

Words and power. The power of words to shape, direct, control. The power to charm, to enlighten, to confuse. The limitless capacity of language to define and prescribe what life means, what life is; to make place for some things and exclude others. The way the stories we tell about ourselves define how we are seen, and what we are allowed to do. And to be. The great streams of talk that *are* the world: the social and political world. More than anything else this flow of words, the sinuous shapes of sentences, a fervent tense, a careful copula – language – has made my life what it is, and what it's worth.

I have no cause for surprise; I'm a writer. But what does surprise are the *ways* in which language has shaped the pattern of my life. Even here in my silent apartment the tangle of words comes to snare me.

Sparkle. A "v" made of red bricks. Plumes of breath on winter air. The tracks of leopards. Excess. Queen of Paris. Body. Bodies. Wind revived and lively. The shape of things that lie across a road. And the road is a path, irregular snaking along the edge of a bay on which slight ships tremble. The road ends at a lighthouse....

Enough. There is still more to go over. I think I will take the last bit of cocaine; the gas is making me sleepy. That's better.... The room seems brighter now. On the wall, one of E.'s little drawings takes on renewed existence. A diminutive girl drinks from a horn nearly as tall as she, staining her lips as she struggles to part them in the dim environs of a clam-shell chamber lined with toy soldiers, all with their backs turned to us. Will she succeed? Will she speak?

The path leads to her room. In a tall building, in a city of tall buildings. A city made of horn and basalt and gold.

In my room meanwhile, the dust on the mirror seems to glitter with pink. And the space seems more crowded. I can almost see my invisible voices. There are five...no six of them tonight. Slender. Medium height. Their clothes are ludicrous: one wears a suit, a kind of dark armor; one an elaborate ball gown with a headpiece shaped like a swan; another a white undershirt and a pair of tight-fitting trousers made of blue serge de Nîmes. I can see none of their faces; those are cloudy, change subtly, but constantly. Their mouths are circles of darkness: holes. Gaping non-spaces that swallow all the specificities of the speaker. Voids in the human space. Termini.

And they are gone; the images never last. My room looks empty once again.

I am alone with the echoes of words. The repetitions of their power and the traces of effects. I always have been and in that solitude I have learnt everything I know about the power of language, because words do have effects; there's no bigger lie than to claim that something is "just words." Language can veil and unveil, can delight or damage. It can do or undo. The power to speak is the power to make change, to determine what happens.

The rich and powerful friends with whom I have whiled away my nights certainly know this. Language serves their absurd distinction with real efficiency. And hedges their privilege with protection. Contrivances like the honorifics that must be used in addressing them, for example. The noticeable, deliberate elegance of their French sets them apart, tests who belongs and who does not. Sometimes I remember with shame how I used a facile verbal dexterity to make a place at their tables or in their salons. Talk brought me into their circles: my writing in the press caught the eye of influential hostesses, the glib table talk I cultivated during my months on the prowl with Eugene as well, but once I was in their pampered quarters, I was astounded by how much of their position was already bound up with speech.

A wedding day is burned into my memory as the very model of this. I went as N.'s escort; Eugene, her usual walker, was in a snit. It was a bright day in the late spring; of course, the ceremony took place in a cathedral, and the reception in a splendid private park. The bride's gown was pristinely white, beautifully

cut to her shape, stretched out in a train of such rare construction that one couldn't possibly say it dragged behind her: it
flowed. Her veil was sheer enough to be the merest suggestion of a veil and it highlighted the sublimity of her face; cast a
greater luminescence on it. The groom was handsome, upright,
and insanely wealthy. Everyone said it was an "excellent match."
Everyone said it and said it. The repetition was striking, as if
the affirmation was a necessary part of the wedding. As if the
statement, in and of itself, created the fact. Which of course, it
did. And as if the clear observation of the fact was as central to
the solemnization of the rite as the priest's intonation of "I now
pronounce you."

I came to understand my speculations were not excessive.
Marriages are, among my fancier friends, *negotiations*. Just as,
to tell the truth, were many areas of their lives. And negotiations are always about talk.

All day the conversations unfolded with a formality that rivaled the wedding liturgy itself. In the garden, over cocktails,
one heard:

The families must be so pleased

What a difference such a marriage will make

The possibilities of such a couple. Imagine!

It is all anyone has been talking about for weeks.

It was too mad. Too much. And never a word about the people, the man and woman joined in this bazaar. The talk swirled
around me, a violent strategizing rather than a fête. N., at one
point, leaned close to say "He brings her family a mountain of
cash they badly need. Her parents, on the other hand, have
a nearly magical power to open any door in Europe.... They
should be very happy together." And she lit a violet cocktail
cigarette.

More of this was made clear to me when dinner was served;
the father's toast rang with evocations of "bold beginnings"
and "infinite possibilities" more the rhetoric of a new business
venture than the celebration of his daughter's new life. I heard

them talk their careful talk, trade their valuable insights, heard them negotiate the shape of my country, and the shape of the future and it made my mouth dry. Their diction was careful; they spoke with flattened, willfully universal accents, they held forth in a blank labyrinth of conversation in which everything was accomplished by saying absolutely nothing as if the unspoken, the implied was a force of nature, a given.

I reeled at the contrast with the hours I spent at the Cyrano, shouting and laughing and arguing and plotting the total destruction of civilization in the company of the surrealists. The passion with which we spoke the word "insurrection" and the desperation with which we sought some way to commit ourselves to the process of change. I heard the screaming and declamations of our long cocktail-hour "meetings," and wondered what the effect of all those words might be. Where might they act? And would they?

And I remembered the many chic dinners, cocktail parties, soirees, lavish country weekends I had spent with these privileged wedding guests during which I talked and laughed and gossiped with the same abandon, made jokes, and puns, with unabashed directness. How they had laughed, volubly and happily, and now, I wondered with teeth clenched what they'd meant by that. But I knew at that wedding that I was welcome among them for one reason only. I was a not friend. I was not diverting company. I wasn't even a decorative, droll touch. That implies some value. I was not amusing. I merely distracted them; in their eyes I was a creature so foreign as to be ridiculous: a clown.

I imagined Eugene at home stubbornly refusing to be at the wedding, but – I knew – miserable for missing it and my heart sunk for him. I went home early.

Four or five days later I saw the Surrealists at the Cyrano and swallowed their talk of revolution like a man dehydrated. I was drunk on it. For four hours I worked at another model of the world with a coterie of committed madmen: one in which the act of speaking was a treasure itself and not a wall around a hoarded treasure. These painters and poets were no less elitist than the wedding party, but they were an accessible elite, indeed one that was out in the streets and bars to recruit. Over the years the group's seriousness about their revolutionary talk had continued to grow, and though the relationship was difficult and involved more jockeying for position than was healthy, their ties with the radical left were real. There were meetings, tracts, angry letters to the editors of various journals, declarations of principle and clarifications of positions proffered and demanded. It was always a struggle, but I believed the relationship was valuable; it was one that could make all of our idealistic rhetoric more real, that would allow the visions of artists to anchor themselves in the world. More and more this belief was shared by other Surrealists.

There are ways of living beyond sincerity. Ambitious ways, rooted in longing. That rise from hope. In a nation of domes, dotted with lights you find one.

A line of people, young and old, male and female, spiral around a raised and inclined apparatus. The line goes on and on, comprised of thousands. And thousands more in the dome down the road. And in the one beyond that. This goes on day and night without surcease.

One by one the people climb the tilted platform to stand under lights and, struggling for balance, tell the story of their life. It is understood by all, everyone standing in the domed room and waiting, or watching on some distant screen at home because they have not yet taken their turn, or have and failed, or are resting between the series of turns they wish to take, that this is not the tale of the life they live, but of the one they most desire. The unlived life that consumes them.

An elderly woman recounts her years of pastry making, of crafting cakes and confections of baroque design and uncommon size for the delectation of children celebrating their rites of passage. Tears are in her eyes as she describes their awestruck laughter and unself-conscious joy.

A man whose age is unclear outlines a twenty-year career in the underground. An insurrectionist, his commitment has seen fires set and pitched battles in suburban bars. He leans heavily on his left leg, concerned about toppling down the sloped stage before he is done.

A boy, scarcely out of school, tells us about love.

Figure after figure takes the platform and empties out his heart – heart-rendingly and without a trace of fact – as if the world depended on it. And it does.

The people of this land will cover those who succeed here in wealth and adulation. In some cases, even with power, because they are sure of almost nothing, but this: whether truth or falsehood, naked or covered in a costume, the world is best left in the hands of the strongest dreamers.

Regardless of that, costume or no, this affiliation with the leftists, and even with the Party, was both a dream and vital force for the surrealists and I, but it was one I feared could tear the group apart. This prospect worried me even though I had formally distanced myself from the group. Disaffiliation aside, I believed in their vision profoundly; it was the one new, powerful possibility for the embittered world left standing after the war. I had seen nothing with more promise, nothing with more beauty and life. So, when I was asked to lend a hand in this tug of war with the "organized left" and give a talk on the group's ideas to a workers' league, I accepted readily, happy for a chance to share my love of this vision and confident it could, if given the chance, spread like a benign virus, orgiastically reproducing in the social body, healing its wounds and sharpening its eyes and ears. Not an illness, but a mutation, giving us wings, and hearts strong enough to let them beat and propel us into the sky.

I left my apartment on the night of my talk swollen with optimism. The evening was warm, so I walked to the hall. Overhead – a perfect omen – the moon was sickle in the sky, and waxing. The men and women of Paris passed me on the narrow sidewalks busy with their lives and I, out of character, brightened with happiness.

The hall where I was to give my talk was in a basement. It was long, and more tight than narrow. There were various unionist posters hanging on the wall: trophies of old battles, slogans for new ones. How, I thought, was an audience used to rhetoric like that going to respond to the message I wanted to deliver? My initial optimism faltered, but I remained certain of the power in my visionary notes.

The evening's organizer came to greet me when I entered. Shook my hand. He was thin, pale-eyed and unexpectedly formal; his stiffness was at war with a scarcely contained nervous energy. He asked politely after André and B., the two members of our group with whom he was most familiar. He sat on committees with them. I told him they were well and that they sent their best wishes. He took this as an end to the niceties, and explained to me that there would be a first speaker who would briefly go over some current business and provide a short report on another committee's meeting, and then the balance of the evening would be given to my speech and a question period. I said thank you and sat down.

As promised, the first speaker shared some news about relations with the Party, the arrest of two organizers a few weeks earlier and the dates foreseen for their trials. He spoke clearly, forcefully, he was youthful and animated, so engaging one *wanted* to listen. As he spoke I saw a selection of surrealists drift into the auditorium. They entered quietly, took seats among the workingmen and women. It surprised and pleased me that they were not easily distinguishable. At least not from the members of the audience who were not dressed in their work clothes. I felt both less alone and less conspicuous.

Then I took the lectern.

I looked out at the room: there were several dozen faces staring up at me. I tried to find some shared feature among them, some mutually assured expression, anything that might make them a single entity to which I could speak directly. There were only rows of distinct visages, idiosyncratic gazes, bodies and faces stirred by their own need, their own dreams. Their own long, hungry wait and I wondered what I could say to satisfy so much, and so much difference.

So I stayed silent for a second longer than I should have. And I started speaking.

"Ladies and Gentlemen, good evening. I have been asked to speak to you about the significance of surrealism for the revolutionary workers' movement. However, standing here before you this evening, I find myself unable to do so in the way in which I had originally intended. It seems imperative first to talk about you, or rather us, each of us, about the lives we live, and the lives we might live."

The faces in the room twitched. The men and women of the Workers' League were clearly used to hearing more theoretical propositions from the stage. The surrealists present, despite their acquaintance with the group's constant debate, were surprised by the sudden change of program.

The stunned looks goaded me on. I told them: the surrealist project is inseparable from life. It begins in our daily experience and our nightly dreams. Its sources are there, and from there grow its objects and its ideas. Anyone who has ever walked down a rain-strewn street and found the pale shadows of imaginary lovers shimmering in the gloss made by street lamps on shallow puddles has had a first glimpse of this. Surely none of us has not encountered a door somewhere that stopped us in our tracks, flooded us with scorching, uncontainable passion to know what lies behind it. You – like I – have surely seen the shape of some problem in life suddenly unfold, or unravel, in a dream, or heard a voice in the night make you a promise. One you believed in. Find that voice in yourself now.

In the third row, a surrealist nodded and whispered to his neighbor. A teenage boy in a printer's uniform slowly licked his lips; they were scarlet.

Surrealism, I said, is dedicated to uncovering these things, exploring them and, most importantly, reshaping the world so it can accommodate, no…so it may *nurture* them. The surrealist revolution is hot in pursuit of a society in which men and women are free to live lives of liberty, enriched experience, pleasure and the meaningful pursuit of their desires. And this means, perforce, the transformation of all alienated social relationships and the exploitation of labor. Everything must change in order to create a world conducive to the human potential for deeper, richer living. It is for this reason that surrealism aligns itself with the workers' movement, sees itself as inseparable from it, because it demands more of the world's real riches for those that create them.

I found my voice beginning to race, my eyes jumped from face to face in the crowd. A blonde woman, young, almost a girl, her glasses slightly askew. An old man halfway back, his hair gray and flattened against his head by the cap he'd worn all day. There was my surrealist pal, P., dapper-looking in the crowd, two fingers stroking his sharp chin. The young man who spoke before me, frankly, openly, staring. I rushed on.

The transformation of economic relations, the phrase stuck in my throat, bristling, of the way in which we worked, day in and day out, merely to survive could never be enough, if life itself was still conceived of as merely a nexus for labor. Any kind of human dignity required more than that.

Imagine, I said, a world built for your desires, for your enjoyment, for the actualization of your dreams and pleasures, and their proliferation. A time and place in which the sensual and intellectual functions of work were given as much value as the instrumental requirements. Imagine a land where public spaces are decorated and work places gilded. A city designed as much for leisure as for labor because there was no difference detectable between them. I spoke on; my voice shook as I came to understand that I was speaking *my own dreams* in the hope that they were shared. Because despite their utopian absurdity they were simple enough, they were human and I knew in the deep and ringing chambers of my heart that they were beautiful.

"Imagine a world," I said and stumbled. Visions caught in my throat, dreams on my teeth. I could feel the water rising in my eyes and my tongue thickening. But I found my way and went on, imagine a different world, I repeated. The straight avenues and highways are pushed to the periphery and the heart of the city given over to winding paths, cul-de-sacs, courtyards. White marble and streaked on the frontage of ordinary buildings, pointless corners that open on patches of green. There is no street without a garden, no garden without a monument to sensual pleasure. A world whose proud capitals are made for walking and for resting, rather than for efficiency; for the delights of wasted afternoons, secret rooms, sudden discoveries and for clandestine pleasures you can share or enjoy alone. The highest towers on the continent stretch themselves into the clouds but are intended not simply to make the most of space, but are crowned with steel aerials and generators that tug lighting out of the sky and bounce it from tower to tower in a display that stops the night walker below and leaves them sighing. A great spectacle of dancing lights unfolds overhead on every summer night. And on the longest night of the year, we tease ourselves with false dawns, artificial daybreaks for the giddy laughter of anticipation. Imagine a civilization, at last a *civilization*, in which work, our labor, was arranged to produce the needful rather than a profit, a world like that is one that could afford such pleasures and one in which millions would work less and none *toil*. One in which everyone, and not merely the rich could *play*.

One might bring together friends in a room, any room. No matter whether it is yours or another's. Rearrange the furniture. Test the positions of chairs and chesterfields and find the one most favorable to conversation or debate or carnal congress. Burn incense and perfumes and scented candles. Set the lighting. The combination of chairs facing away from the sofa is called the Room of the Father. The odor of storax is in the air. An alignment of the seating with the low table across the room, this is the Room of the Hare. A greener scent summons. This is the way worlds are made. Choices and oppositions. Out of play and out of calculation.

Indeed. That world is the meeting place of the workers and the surrealists I said: our forum, our public square. Its realization is why we must work together to change life and to remake the world, because, in the deepest sense, the most useful one, those two things, as my friend André Breton has written are, for us, but one.

I stopped there. I looked out at my listeners again. Their faces were blank, silent and somehow brilliant. Little rows of pale stars, glowing in the dim hall. A microcosm. A fleshly, fractured galaxy in miniature. Some mouths were half open. Lips parted; they could be forming questions, or catching their breath...or stunned into wordlessness. Their faces – those moons, those suns – bright things clustered together in the artificial gloom. I saw two surrealists seated side by side and wearing identical smiles. Indecipherable. I saw a man in his fifties, blinking rapidly, a telegraph flashing me a message I could not understand, shifting in his seat as if he could not contain himself. A few rows back, a young woman whose angular haircut told me more about her commitment to being absolutely modern than I could possible hear, merely stared, hard. The silence was filled with small movement, but was resolute. And it stretched, while I stood alone, pinned to the stage by a spotlight, a kind of long-spoken butterfly watching the life drain from it, counting the measured, slowing beats of my wings.

Finally, it broke, and a woman still dressed in the grey uniform of a city worker rose and spoke. She spoke in a plain, blunt voice, one that cracked and strained, a blend of exhaustion at the end of her day and confusion at what she had just heard. She asked me a question about practical matters: how workers could even begin to target such a goal, about how one could even conceive of so total a transformation when even one's time was not one's own, when many bosses resisted recognizing even legal and religious holidays.

Soundlessness retook the hall when she ended. No one whispered to his neighbor now. No one uncrossed his legs, or turned in her seat. No door creaked or wind struck a window. And, the last movements in my lepidopterous wings drained away leaving them limp. I had no answer for her. My mind spun, but I found nothing. Below me, the stage transmogrified, became viscous as muck, red and grey; its foul odor filled my nostrils as shame crept across my brow. I saw faces I recognized from the Cyrano regarding me blankly, the eyes of strangers measured me and waited. With a vast effort, I pulled one of my feet from the swamp in my imagination and took a step back on the stage, away from the eyes and tried to speak.

I answered as I could; tried to make bridges between ends and means and discovered they functioned imperfectly. I struggled to not appear awkward, not sound ridiculous. With every syllable that fell from my mouth, I felt compromise clinging to me, ripping and tearing: a flesh eating plant sprung from the swamp at my feet.

Choking on my sense of failure, I forced out a discussion of the relationship of vision and praxis, the need for a sense of the goal in order to shape useful tools for achieving it, an explanation of the differences and the connections between the kind of work a union could do, and that envisageable by the surrealist group, about the need to struggle for the liberation of the mind and the factory at once. I told the echoingly quiet room that the development of strategies was a separate process; one best entered collectively, to ensure that they both met the needs of the movement, and mirrored its values. I talked about solidarity even as I wanted to run from the podium, plunge headlong into the darkened streets and forget myself, the evening, and the world in the deepest part of my magical park just a few metro stops away.

Even as I spoke I knew I was uttering half-truths and eva- sions. I loved the vision I had outlined with every nerve and synapse, every drop of blood in me, but the truth was I had no idea of how to achieve it, and have heard the thousand thou- sand ways it could be waylaid, diverted, destroyed narrated to me countless times by my invisible voices. I loved it and knew, or almost knew, that it was doomed. My passion and my hopes were at war in me and though the struggle stirred, it savaged too. Without the tools, how does one ever climb the walls of heaven anyway?

Nonetheless, the young woman who asked me her question seemed mollified if not satisfied. She nodded. She sat down. I saw that whispering pair of surrealists settle back in their seats looking at least a little calmer.

A few more questions were asked. Some easier to answer, but none reassured me, none lit a spark of hope and set my op- timism afire once more. I answered methodically, committed to seeing what I had promised André through. I would represent the group's positions as best I could. But I was shaken. Deeply and hard.

Still, there were moments I saw the day laborers and lines- people in the room share some of my excitement, saw they still clung to their own dreams and hopes. So I held to that, when I could. I told myself that at least incomprehension is a blank slate to start from.

By the end of the evening, I had almost convinced myself of it.

Just before I left the stage, I noticed one more face in the crowd. A young man, blonde and handsome. He stood up to speak, then sat back down again, not once, but twice. Twice he rose to his feet, his determination to say something clear on his face and twice he sat down, unable to express what he wanted to. A tendon near my shoulder quivered both times. I knew just how he felt. And there was nothing I could do.

I left the hall confused. And spoke to no one on the way out. But I was spoken to.

The shock and uncertainty of the evening brought my voices back to me. This one was harsh, yet seductive, forceful but not aggressive. It sounded relentless and patient at the same time. It would make its point. Oh, yes. It would.

Yes. Yes. I remember it too. There. And there. I spoke to you about the road ahead, the angles and the ends. The turns and towers. Here is a world to love and to fear because everything is offered to you. Sit in a chair and be served Sweet Boy. All of the world's knowledge rushed to you, rendered. Tiny bits of news and boxes filled with pleasant information. Endless streams of faces, voices, words washed over everyone carrying news of the latest decisions of world governments, the death of a beloved singer, the weather for the next three days, the size of new-born orangutan in a zoo on the far side of the continent, the height of a new monument, the color of the fabrics to move down the world's runways next year, the average debt burden of an entire people, the release dates of new films, an endlessly repeated refrain torn from a popular song, the murder rate in the city in which one's sister has gone to live, the passage of new legislation, the conduct of a second war, on a second front, the name of a man, uncommonly young, appointed to the supreme court, the wreck of a ship and the spread of its cargo in a fragile ocean somewhere, the discovery of a new cure, the failure of a company, despair in the suburbs and the rioting fury of the young, a treaty signed, a treaty broken. This will surely stir you, Friend. A rush, an interminable rush of data phrased and communicated in the most compelling ways and whole populations, taking it in. You can take it in forever, no need to stop, constantly renewed sweetnesses and fresh horizons. You need never stop, need never weigh one thing against the next because there is always more. Always more. And more. No

*need to fuss over meaning when information is constantly re-
newed.*

*No learning, here, only information. Information freed. In-
formation free.*

*Nor does your pleasure stop there, because you too, my sad and
lonely interlocutor, are information too. You too are watched.
Fascinated eyes in a hemisphere shrouded by night, will watch
you as you shave, will read your books and praise or immolate
them. Found and judged in the space of a heartbeat. Images of
you consumed like dry candy by strangers. Your name a token
and a trading card. Your movements and emotions swallowed
up. Every cough calculated, every tear recorded. A twitch in
the eyebrow isolated and run through a series of precise tests to
unveil its hidden burden of signification. Nothing unperceived,
nothing not meaningful, but never any sense. This is information, not exchange.*

A rush of sound and suggestion, like you. Even the quiet of
my stunned audience that night is preferable. At least there was
some unanimity: they were open-mouthed, their eyes wider
than when I had begun. There was some nobility at least in
that.

I know because there have been other times my talk was less
noble. Bent to less worthy ends. Too many such times. Once,
it was at a costume ball – there must be four or five such evenings in a year, the wealthy love a mask – I caught myself almost ready to let drop one of the tales my spectral companions
shared with me.

It was at the home of a young couple that were both children of old families, who had "literary" and "artistic" tastes, so a
number of surrealists, like André, L. and M. were there, despite
an "official" disinclination for fashionable company. The soiree
itself had a vaguely literary theme turning around the middle
ages. Or perhaps it was more gothic than that, Hugo's *Notre-
Dame de Paris*. I have forgotten the specifics because other
memories have come to dominate my sense of the night.

The place was elaborately decorated with faux brick walls and turrets and long stretches of painted canvas mimicking tapestry. High in the corners shields blazoned with coats of arms – that may well have been real, given our hosts – presided over the crowd. On long trestle tables food was presented with savage grandeur, while liveried servants wandered back and forth for those too engaged to serve themselves. There were candles too, clustered on benches, on stands, on long posts of wood. All safely out of the way of the outlandish ensembles favored that evening.

I drank a little too much, and enjoyed myself a great deal in the earlier part of the evening. It was then that Eugene arrived with N., with whom I still lunched from time to time. Our affair was long over, but I was still pleased to see him. The two were dressed in monastic robes made of thick red velvet and trimmed in some sort of fur. I am sure that N. paid the tailor. We talked while the band built itself to a raucous pitch, joined by a group of American jazzmen. We traded on our confidences, built a small world for just the three of us that lasted as long as the pleasure we took in each other's company. Eugene was painting even less but seemed more beautiful than ever. I was saddened by the realization that neither of those things affected me now. My nights now were different from those of our shared months. They left me to dance. Eugene touched my chest as he departed. It felt lovely.

I watched the crowds swirl higher.

Where were they going? There are crowds here that move in time to music, rapid waves of men and women. There. There. A city of people whose only function is to move, animating different neighborhoods in an endlessly deferred conflict, a planned and bloodless battle, since they themselves are the enemy they seek; not finding anyone to fight they hurry to the next quarter of the city.

Not that crowd in motion. These merely drank and danced and laughed and imagined the whole world did the same. As

Eugene and N. took to the dance floor, a young woman came running up to me, dressed in a parodic, and couture, version of some gypsy dancing girl's attire. She threw her arms around me squealing my name, kissed me wetly on both cheeks lamenting – with laughter – the great lapse of time since we had last seen each other. Taking my hand she pulled me towards a corner to gossip about a new business initiative of her father's involving a daily newspaper and a new young man she had met. She was eager to know if I had seen him anywhere in my nightly excursions; she had no way of knowing how much less frequent they had become. I was about to reassure her when a drum roll tore through the hall. Long, thunderously bass, persistent. A space opened in the middle of the room as uniformed figures asked us to move back. Risers were carried in, and a tall, gilded chair.

They sat there for a moment alone, and braziers were brought in to flank the throne on either side. All of the conversation in the immense ballroom fell dead. Banners were brought out and held aloft along the sides of the open space; pink and gold and a garish, citrusy green. On each of them was embroidered a gleeful face: a whole array of clowns, court fools in motley and belled caps, *commedia dell'arte* Punchinellos, circus caperers from a hundred years back. One had sequined eyes that seemed to wink in the semi-light. Another's broad grin was so crimson it was bloody. Three in a row had pale silk skin: ivory white, the yellow of diamonds, a pink as translucent as a drop of grenadine in sparkling water. Smiling clowns. Laughing crowns. Clowns roaring open-mouthed with jaws that swallow every chaos. Mad. Glad. All held aloft by the row of servants.

The young lady left me as a man took the impromptu stage to stand before the vacant seat. He was dressed in a ragged-looking robe with a chasuble atop it. A dented triple tiara rested on his head. Even from my distance I could tell his "rags" too were fine fabrics, silks as lavish as those of the banners and his "patches" were sewn by hand and beaded with skill. A white

woolly beard was glued to his chin. It trembled as he gestured
in the air. Blessing us all.

Two young women cross-dressed as pages with matching
eye-patches came out to blow a fanfare. They tilted back their
heads and the great bell-mouths of the horns set loose a sound
that shook the ceiling's plaster *putti*.

The hobo-pontiff started to speak, "My Lords and Ladies,"
he begins. I forced the smirk from my face; in that chamber,
with those guests, the opening was more than a rhetorical
flourish. "Welcome to our Court, it is my pleasure, one shared
I am certain by our generous hosts, to welcome you again and
to encourage you to eat, drink and be merry. In the spirit of this
evening's frolics, and in my role as your Convener, it is my most
agreeable duty to call upon you to celebrate the folly to which
we render homage tonight with all due ceremony." He pauses,
"Let us proceed to the election of a King to preside over our
revelries!" My head ached; they were creating a court of fools.

Most of my fellow guests, however, were less contemptuous.
A wave of applause surged through the crowd. A little flutter
of silvery laughter came from some ladies who were already im-
portuning their escorts as the well-established rituals of their
class required. I was relieved to be back from the centre of the
action. I took another cup of champagne from a passing waiter;
something sparkling seemed the right choice for the evening's
entertainment.

Our tattered Convener continued, encouraging those prepared to compete for the crown to come forward and make
their claim. More applause, louder laughter. A man dressed as
a bandit rushed to the centre of the floor. A cloak of fur was on
his shoulders, a bold helmet on his head; his beard was waxed
to a sharp point that echoed the sword he brandished. He
slashed, cut the air and began to declaim an account of idiot
exploits: the sacking of a haystack, a ravaged olive grove and
a great night of drinking with a gang of trolls. The assembled
revelers laughed and applauded the account. He leapt about

the floor stabbing into emptiness as he recounted his vicious struggle with an abandoned wagon – which was clearly the sorcerously camouflaged form of a vile wizard. He tripped, re-covered, slashed at the hallucinatory veiled wagonwheel-head of the mage.

"Enough of this," shouts another man as he strides on to the dance floor. He is disguised as a hugely bloated harlequin; some hidden apparatus of struts and bent wire shaping the parti-col-ored suit into a nearly perfect sphere. His legs, reduced to shins and feet, clad in mismatched pointed shoes, protrude from the globular body's lower half. "Simple delusions are not sufficient to our purpose. Surely the kind of folly we enjoy should be ruled over by a greater fool than this!" He grabs at his spherical faux belly for emphasis. The gesture sends the whole mecha-nism of his torso shaking. "Allow me to make my case," and he begins a tale.

The inflated harlequin, sated with a fine dinner one evening, set out to find a sympathetic tavern in which to enjoy his post-prandial digestive. His quest took him into an unfamiliar street (not surprisingly, he said, since he so rarely left his home, and when he did he was almost inevitably chauffeured.) He became worried about finding his way back. To avoid this, he decided to mark his trail, but, recalling the tales of foolish children who had attempted as much with breadcrumbs only to find them eaten by birds, decided to do so with coins. Thus, he planned to thwart nature's annoyances. He proceeded this way some short time until he came across what seemed to him a charming little bistro. As he opened the door, he was surprised to see a crowd of almost a dozen close behind him, their hands filled with his coins. And to learn that he no longer had enough in his pock-ets to pay for his port, much less the libations awaited by the crowd drawn by his largesse during the journey.

The guests roared at the story; none of us yet knew how the financial disaster spreading across the world would rip the hu-mor from the tasteless joke. In the gale of hilarity, I heard a

softer remark. "These people are an offense." A sentence so unexpected that I thought it was one of my voices at first. Then I
saw the speaker from the corner of my eye and turned to face
him. The high brow, the combed-back mane, the green velvet
jacket were unmistakable, despite the mask he wore with its
pattern of grey stone, crenellations, and battlements that transformed his face into a fortress: a defense for his contempt. It
was André by my side. My face brightened involuntarily at the
sight of him, perhaps my first genuine smile of the evening.

"You are, of course, right." I answered.

"Why do I suspect you of humoring me, René?"

"Because you are too suspicious, my friend."

He shrugged, put his arm around my shoulder to pull me
into a conspiratorial closeness. He whispered.

"Look at them," he said. "They play like children in a palace."

On the floor before us more men, and some women, had
scampered forward to caper and act like idiots. A good-looking
young man walked on his hands, while behind him two more
leap-frogged towards a fine bronze sculpture. Everywhere the
signs of a long suppressed, hysteria bubbled free, visibly building to some cataclysmic point. The laughter was shriller now,
shouts and exhortations joined it. Bursts of machine-gun applause. The clown-pope shouted encouragement and waved
his arms from his improvised dais. I saw two men dressed in
a shared dragon costume rush onto the floor to leap on a man
dressed as a knight. To devour him? To fuck him?

André's bile poured out, righteous, acute, analytically dazzling and sometimes a shade short of compassion. But never
quite wrong. He decried the excess, the expense, the self-indul-
gence, the way that this entire riot parodied anything like real
joy. "They chase pleasure without understanding it," he said.
"They run after it desperately and know no satisfaction because
they haven't gone without often enough to know that half of
any pleasure lies in its pursuit."

A man in motley rushed past us, chased by a woman with a large purple bow who kept dropping her arrows.

I looked at the room, as frenzied in its way as the hidden corners of my park at night, but without any of its silence, any of its deliberateness. Too giddy, merely. Without its fanfare of sobs to join the chorus of shouts. André was right. I tilted my head against him, and he squeezed my shoulder. But there was more to it than that. The horror went deeper. All of the shrill pleasure was not a search for limits, not a splintering of the formality and plenty of their lives; it was a bulwark built around it. They spent without real loss and so learned nothing from it. It was a placeholder for boredom, a valve for their hopes. I felt sick. And I felt rich.

"André," I simply said, "It's worse than that. They're the only people in the world with enough power to play at giving it up."

His laugh was short, deep. A kind of bark.

The tattered Pope pulled a man to the stage: our king was found. The pontiff placed a crown of tin on his head. I saw a swath of red on his chin. But I saw it very briefly as the drunken sovereign teetered round to drop his trousers and show his subjects his ass.

André and I had had enough at this point. We turned to leave, with him whispering to me about a café not too far away that might still be open, where we might stop for a nightcap, have a moment to catch up. The idea tempted me.

As we headed for the doors, I saw a tall, fair waiter staring at me as he refilled a tray. His pale eyes shined, as intense as the tip of a knife cutting through the silky air: to expose flesh, or to cut it? There was something familiar about him, his focus was ferocious and uncommitted at the same time. He didn't take a step towards me, only stared. Then, ever so quickly he turned away, and turned back almost immediately to stare again and I remembered. The pale young man was the same one who repeatedly stood to speak and sat down at my talk in the basement hall. That hesitant beautiful youth who struggled with his conscience. Struggling again, with bearding or abandoning me. I turned to approach him, hoping to make it easier, more comfortable for him to say whatever it was he wanted to. I felt André's hand on my shoulder. "Here," he said, "They've brought us our coats." In the moment I thanked him, the young waiter was gone, vanished into the masked crowds, laboring under his tray.

We made our way into the night, and a bar, and a long, lovely conversation, but the image of that young man, his twitchiness, his earnest look, his heartbreaking indecision clung to me, because I had seen so much uncertainty, had lived with it myself. And would see more.

I wrestled, too, with its darker twin, an odious and fierce certainty, an arrogant assuredness; my most recent encounter with which is where this tale must come to its end: the last two days. My last two days. In some ways, everything leads to this. My various talks and interventions, my writing and journalism, my surrealist activities and the stream of silent stories have all brought me here: an impossible knot, an untenable point of intellectual and ethical conflict.

Over the last weeks a committee, on which I sit, has been working on a Conference of radical writers and intellectuals "for the Defense of Culture." I entered the work honestly enough, seeing it as a normal next step. But, it's always a mistake to think of steps, of decisions, as normal. Every one is extraordinary. Every decision is an exception. Though they always lead somewhere, it is rarely where one thinks.

The conference is a response to the dangerous political situation that's developed since the stock market crash. All of us see Hitler's rise in Germany and the increasing radicalism of the right here in France as threats that must be confronted; the stakes for intellectual life in Europe are greater than they have ever been. Everywhere, one sees signs of a leveling of thought and public discourse, a praising of the least challenging ideas and positions, often of the sheerest stupidity. Politicians call it the voice of the "common man," as if ordinary citizens were incapable of reason. The reduction of clear analysis to catchphrases is commonplace; freedom versus treason, good versus evil, the glory of the republic versus the barbarian hordes that threaten it. Every newspaper, book or play is pressured down, reduced to the level of the lowest common denominator until there is no meaningful difference between them, every utterance is viewed as having the same weight and value whether it is a xenophobic harangue in a cheap newspaper or a novel from a leading man of letters. The will to ignorance is omnipresent.

Even worse, the plague of stupidity is mated to one of violence; the streets of Paris, the same streets I've wandered by night in search of wonders and pleasures, have been the scene of violent battles between fascist thugs and communists. I've seen bloody cobblestones fly through the air. A man with a blackened and crushed eye has run into me as he rounded a corner in flight. I hid him in the backroom of a café while nationalist brutes shouted for him to come out.

Slogans surround us these days, and strong arms to translate them into action. People go in fear of speaking their minds and truths. We who speak as a trade must speak louder now.

For weeks I've sat in tiny rooms arguing about focus and procedure, cobbling this conference together, and fighting long and hard to make a place at the table for the surrealists. The opposition I faced was enormous. André's reputation for being difficult (and that of his friends for being rowdy) is no small stumbling block. My recent resignation from the "formal" group has helped though, lending me credibility, granting me an impartial aura and eliminating perceived conflicts of interest.

The work, though tedious for stretches, felt important. As the gathering is "international" I worked once more with old friends like T. and a host of new acquaintances: writers from Belgium, Britain and Germany itself were taking part, as well as a formidable contingent from the triumphant revolutionary USSR, one that included E., the author of a tract that openly insulted the surrealists. It disparaged their work, their politics, their morals and the seriousness of their engagement with politics and the left. The day it came to André's attention, he reeled with anger at the imputations of degeneracy, fetishism and – worst of all in his eyes – pederasty. Needless to say, E.'s presence on the committee created a legion of difficulties for me.

Over many long meetings I watched E. sit in his chair, looking comfortable, head pulled back as he surveyed the discussions with drowsy eyes. There is a mist of confidence, or self-assuredness around him. One that must have a sedative effect since his head would scarcely move when a new speaker intervened. He was not silent, however. He commented from time to time, never rudely, never too forcefully. He had no need to push. He represented the writers of the one country on the planet to have seen a successful socialist revolution. In that cramped room, his moral authority felt absolute. Outside the room, one occasionally heard less admiring comments.

Over the weeks I managed to sway the committee towards giving the surrealists a place at the Congress; in particular, André would be allowed to speak. My sense of triumph was so palpable I glowed. For a day and a night I believed in possibilities again; I forgot the boredom of committee work and saw a freshly laid road, leading towards a brighter future and paved in colored stones. I thought a bridge might be built between the surrealists and the more politicized groups of revolutionary intellectuals; I believed we might work together to counter the hardening positions of the right, might somehow stem the tide of intolerance and violent propaganda churning in our shared culture.

In no time at all, and, through no fault of mine, for once, such hopes were shattered.

André had seen E. in the street, by itself a sure disaster. He could never let an insult slide and the rant about the surrealists was laden with them. I am told that on the fateful afternoon he dashed across a busy street to accost the Russian on the sidewalk. Dodging traffic, he called out in a rage, challenging the slanders he'd read. He shouted, "Do you know me, Sir?" "No," came E.'s answer. André introduced himself, slapping the Russian as he did so. E. denied knowing him again, and André repeated his name accompanied by one of the insulting terms from the article: "I am André Breton, fetishist" or "dilettante" or "degenerate" and slapped him again. The procedure was repeated three times before he was satisfied.

E., of course, would have satisfaction in his turn. And it was simple; he insisted that the surrealists not be allowed to speak at the Congress. Not one of them, and particularly not Breton.

I argued against the decision; the aim of the congress was to bring writers and intellectuals together in opposition to the fascist menace threatening to sweep away any and all culture that would not serve its jingoistic ends. A menace that grew stronger and stronger with every passing day, a flood that could drown everything that's best in the life of the mind. Every hand and mind was needed if we were to draw a line in the sand. I exhausted myself in outlining the vital contributions made by surrealism's explorations of the mind, dreams, language, and how useful they could be in a battle against such willful unknowingness.

To no end. It was pointless. In the meeting room, smoke-filled and fraught, The Russian sat stoically in a chair before the only open window, drowsing as I spent myself in rhetoric. Behind his back, twilight settled on the monuments of Paris; the sun going down in a cascade of red. When I stopped my arguments, he lifted his hand to cover a yawn, blinked once or twice, shook his head to clear it and said, "No," very calmly, and without raising his voice. The surrealists would not speak, or the Soviet delegation would withdraw from the Congress, he repeated himself. The deed was done. There was nothing else to be said; it was inconceivable to hold the Congress without Soviet representation. Impossible. Breton and the rest would not make their presentation. That was the end of it.

In the last few days, I've tried some final desperate stratagems. I've crossed Paris from top to bottom, petitioning my friends to pressure André. Begging them to convince him to apologize. I am too cowardly, or too attached, to ask him myself. I've made dozens of phone calls, knocked on countless doors. "Would Breton excuse himself?" No. And no again. P. argued with him. Others from his inner circle. He hears nothing.

Nor will E. budge. The two men are remorseless, absolutely intractable. Two immovable objects, vast cold icebergs crushing the fragile ship of the Congress between them. But, of course it will go on with or without the impact it might have had; the surrealists will not speak. The debate on our dim hope for salvation will take place without their voices: the voices of dreams, vision, passion and infinite possibilities. The voice of the untamed, the self-justified, the speech of the place beyond productivity. Those voices will be silenced once again.

My head hurts and I wonder why, in all the vertiginous parade of worlds my invisible companions have laid out for me, did they never tell me about a world utterly without hope?

Because we have never seen such a place.

Well, I have. And now, I can do no more. I am tired. And weak. Today the results of my most recent tests arrived. My tuberculosis is back. I'm done.

The congress will happen and it will change nothing. Everything fails. The Hitlerian rabble will rise and continue to rise; I have no doubt that one day it will even reach Paris and stretch out its long, brown, bloodied arm still further. Everything fails. The writers will speak and speak and speak, just like my voices and just as intangible. Just as free of substance. Where is the hope in that?

And you, my speakers, how much can you claim for the worlds you have shown me? Everything fails. A labyrinth of tunnels. A lust for storms. Hands failing to meet through a clear wall. Everything fails. Where is the hope in all that?

In a small room, windowless and walls painted flat black.
Two people in animal masks join hands over a table built
waist high. Behind them a large fish tank glows with a blue
light. There are no signs of movement in the thick water. The
masked pair speaks to each other in a fictional language. It is
rhythmical and sibilant. They are making sense.

Maybe, "hope" is the wrong word. I've struggled all my life to make something perfect, to find an absolute somehow. I've struggled with the great blackness between the word and the act, between beauty and fear, between me, in all my individuality, alone, in my head and in the world, and some other person out there whose heart might sound to the same unperceived music as my own, and I've finally come to understand that the opposites can not be united. That alchemy is a lie. All the promises, all the struggles to remake the world, or to make it anew, are wrong. The oneness of things is in their very opposition, they come together only in action: to fight, or to fuck. They are irresolvable, because their resolution is found only in obliteration.

That is why we rebel, not so much for the faint hope of winning, but to find the breaking point in ourselves and in the world. And this is where mine is, in a room slowly filling with gas and an army of voices that returns to me.

How wide is a world? Blue ink at the crossroads and a larval
form of instinct. Glow in the dark. Time spent. Time paid.
Shudder and sing what remains to you.

I suppose, given how much of my life has been about words, I should say something as I exit. But I have nothing to say really. Let me at least write a note.

"Please cremate my remains." There. No. That is not enough.

"Please cremate my remains. Disgust." There that's it. I'll pin it to my jacket.

Stems stripped of leaves. The passage of time. A wall uninter-
rupted. Glass. And menace.

My old friends. My absent mountainside.

I feel dizzy. I should sit down. What are those lights that cluster together? That sound.

Here. A clock running backwards. Here. Some music you once knew. Here.

How different from when I first heard you. When everything was "there."

Here. Here.

A cloud of something and all you say in the end is "here," "here." It's both an affirmation, like the clamor at a wedding toast, a speech as the masses rise up. And it's a direction too, a way out. A finger pointing at a door.

The sound of someone knocking.

"Who's there?" as L. wrote, all those years ago. Before he put on his inquisitor's robes. "Good. Show in the infinite."

Here. Here.

AUTHOR'S NOTE

This narrative is a work of fiction. Though it may be unnecessary to stress this, the fact that the central character is a historical figure prompts me to make it explicit. I claim no knowledge of Crevel beyond what is in the record; certainly no knowledge of his mind and motivations, or, in particular, of what prompted his suicide. Though some (and by no means, all) of the incidents in *Subtle Bodies* are drawn from what is known of Crevel's life, the account is not biographical, nor is it intended to be. It is a work of the imagination, of, as I said, fiction, and beyond even that, a work of fantastic fiction, created for pleasure rather than information.

Those who are interested in René Crevel, the surrealist group and the cultural and political ferment of Paris in the Twenties and Thirties will find useful information in the many scholarly and critical titles published on the subjects. I can also happily refer those able to read French to Michel Carassou's biography of Crevel. This book does not seek to join the ranks of such scholarly titles; I have written a number of essays on related subjects but the aim of this work is different.

As to why one might choose to make fiction from a historical figure, something I have never done prior to this, there are a number of factors that encouraged me to undertake the project. First, I've read Crevel's work with a great deal of interest and enjoyment. Beyond that, however, one notes among the surrealists at various points in their history, a sharp interest in mythology and in the creation of a modern myth. Consider Breton's concern with the figure of Melusine in *Arcanum 17*, for example, or the emergence of the "Great Invisibles" in the *Prolegomena to a Third Manifesto of Surrealism or Else*. There is something in this quest for a "new myth" that strikes me as vital to the surrealist project, because of all the *avant gardes* to strut through the Twentieth Century none, for better or worse, has captured our culture's imagination in the same way, nor had a similar cultural impact. In some ways – important ways, I might argue – surrealism itself *became* the myth it was seeking; "surreal," after all, is now part of our everyday language. So, perhaps by taking some of Crevel's biography and the history of the Parisian surrealist group and spinning them in new directions, *Subtle Bodies* can take on, not so much the facts of surrealism, as the surrealist myth. At least, I thought it was worth a try.

In closing, I would like to use this opportunity to thank a number of people for their help and kindness during my work on *Subtle Bodies*:

First, Mathieu, for his unwavering love and support. Writing would be a great deal more difficult without it. As would everything else.

My sister, Joy, for being an astute and engaged first reader.

The fabulous Steve Berman, for publishing this novella and for the conversation one steamy afternoon in New Orleans that sparked my work on it.

And you good folks, of course, for taking the time to read the book. I hope you enjoy the trip.

PETER DUBÉ
Montreal, 2010